THE HOUSE OF SHELLS

EFUA TRAORÉ

Chicken House

2 Palmer Street, Frome, Somerset BA11 1DS
www.chickenhousebooks.com

Text © Efua Traoré 2022

First published in Great Britain in 2022
Chicken House
2 Palmer Street
Frome, Somerset BA11 1DS
United Kingdom
www.chickenhousebooks.com

Chicken House/Scholastic Ireland, 89E Lagan Road, Dublin Industrial Estate,
Glasnevin, Dublin D11 HP5F, Republic of Ireland

Cover and interior design by Helen Crawford-White
Typeset by Dorchester Typesetting Group Ltd
Printed and bound in Great Britain by CPI Group (UK) Ltd, Croydon, CR0 4YY

FSC
www.fsc.org
MIX
Paper from
responsible sources
FSC® C171272

1 3 5 7 9 10 8 6 4 2

British Library Cataloguing in Publication data available.

PB ISBN 978-1-913696-71-9
eISBN 978-1-913696-96-2

A joy of a book. Rich, warm, powerful storytelling.
KATHERINE RUNDELL

A magical adventure in a beautiful setting . . .
SOPHIE ANDERSON

I was transported and transfixed from
start to finish! A brilliant debut!
PATIENCE AGBABI

A thrilling adventure bright with the gorgeous
colours of Nigeria – glorious!
JASBINDER BILAN

I really enjoyed this rich, atmospheric magical adventure . . .
KATHERINE WOODFINE

. . . thrilling, precise, expansive, bursting with life and music.
INUA ELLAMS

Gorgeous . . . An enthralling story celebrating the fierce
love of grandmothers, mothers and daughters.
ABI ELPHINSTONE

The fantasy creates tension and drama, but the best
aspect of this book is the evocation of place . . .
Clear, vigorous prose beckons the reader in.
THE SUNDAY TIMES

Traoré's storytelling feels almost otherworldly . . . an exhilarating,
supernatural journey into urban and rural Nigeria.
THE TIMES

[A] wonderful fantasy adventure . . .
Full of atmosphere, it's a richly described story
of beauty, adventure, courage and magic.
THE WEEK JUNIOR

Short   2022

A MESSAGE FROM CHICKEN HOUSE

I love Efua's astonishing writing – she blends legends and beliefs with modern, moving stories of family and friendship. In a forbidden house, Kuki – our heroine – finds a friend when she needs one most. But is this new friend her greatest ally or her worst enemy? Kuki's belief in their friendship could save her from an ancient curse – or kill her if she's wrong. This warm and exciting story full of wisdom and beauty will stay with you long after you turn the last page.

BARRY CUNNINGHAM
Publisher
Chicken House

For Shola, Enina and Leila
I love that you share my love for books
This one, is another one
for you

In vain your bangles cast
Charmed circles at my feet;
I am Abiku, calling for the first
And the repeated time.

Wole Soyinka, 'Abiku'

1

THE WEIGHT OF A NAME

'K o-ku-mo!'

Kuki jerked up, her story notepad dropping out of her hands on to the floor. The page she had been writing on disappeared between the others, along with the wisp of an idea she had just had to save the situation for her heroine.

Aunty's loud voice calling her full name was always a shock. Everyone else called her Kuki.

Kuki struggled out of bed, and hurried towards the kitchen. She already felt guilty even though she was sure she hadn't done anything wrong. Or had she?

Since they had moved into Dr D's house, his sister came round and hovered over them like the

Wicked Witch of the West. Gone were the quiet, cosy times of just Mum and her in their little flat. Even though Kuki wanted to be happy for her mum that she had found a new husband after so many years, sometimes she couldn't help being angry with her for disrupting their lives.

'Yes, Aunty?' she said timidly, sticking her head into the hot kitchen. Her eyes immediately began to water from the thick peppery palm oil fumes that filled the air. Aunty was sitting on a stool at the kitchen table, a shiny gele tied meticulously around her head, her arms and neck covered with glittering jewellery.

'Your mother is pregnant and should be resting,' she said. 'Why are you not here helping her in the kitchen? A big girl like you! Quick, cut slices of yam, two for each person.'

Kuki glanced at her mum who was at the sink washing a bunch of leaves. She had to stretch her arms to reach the tap because her belly was in the way.

Mum rolled her eyes and winked at Kuki. 'I told Kuki to rest because she had a tough week in school,' she said.

Unfortunately, that was the worst thing to have said.

Aunty immediately turned to examine Kuki. 'Are you feeling weak?' she asked, her eyes narrowing.

Kuki shook her head quickly. 'I feel perfectly fine, Aunty. I'll just go get the yam,' she said, hoping that would be the end of the matter. Since the day Aunty had heard that Kuki had been ill when she was a baby and fainted once when she was little, she had begun to act strangely, constantly asking her about how she felt.

Kuki hurried to the small storeroom at the other end of the kitchen and grabbed a yam.

Aunty was rummaging in the glittery handbag on her lap when she returned. 'In fact, I have something for both of you,' she said.

She pulled out a black plastic bag and tore it open. A package of crumpled newspapers fell out with a metallic thump. She began to separate layers of newspaper until a curious heap of metal chains and bangles decorated with feathers and colourful threads, clattered on to the table.

'This is protection for both of you,' Aunty said.

'They are special amulets welded together by a famous Babalawo that my friend recommended.'

'You went to a Babalawo?' Mum asked, her eyes as wide as if they were about to plop out of her head. 'Goodness, Bisola, why would you go to some shady juju man shack to get these?'

'It wasn't a shack and he wasn't shady,' Aunty retorted sharply. 'He had an office which was very well kept. He is a very modern Babalawo.'

'Well, that's even worse,' Mum said, placing her hands on her hips. 'You shouldn't patronize such people. That only keeps such superstitious beliefs alive. And I have told you so many times, we do not need any protection! We are perfectly well and fine, and nothing will happen to us.'

Kuki reached out to pick up one of the bracelets. It had thin red threads intricately woven through a chain with a tiny bell attached to its centre. It actually looked quite pretty. She had never seen anything like it before.

'Kuki! Do not touch those godless things,' Mum cried.

But Kuki's fingers had already stopped in mid-air. The beautiful bracelet had suddenly felt wrong to her – as if it were too bright, too harsh. She shuddered. Were these things really juju?

'Please go to your room, Kuki. I want to talk to your aunt,' Mum said.

'Ahn-ahn, you should take these things seriously, Grace,' Aunty said. 'Why are you being so stubborn? And you should stop calling that child Kuki! Call her by her full name. K-o-k-u-m-o! Remind her every day that she will not die.'

Her words cut through the air like daggers and the usual worry stabbed the inside of Kuki's belly. Not because she was afraid that she would die. She felt strong and full of life and, like her mum, she didn't believe in superstitions. But her name – which meant: 'this one will not die!' – was such an awful reminder for her mum of the time just after her birth, when Kuki had been very ill and spent weeks at the hospital.

Kuki sighed. She wished she hadn't been given such a heavy name to bear, tainted with fear and worry. Her father had given it to her, only to abandon them shortly afterwards.

As she edged towards the door Kuki glanced back nervously.

Her mum looked as if she had just drunk a cup of concentrated, bitter Agbo during a bout of malaria. 'Kuki does not need any reminder of that,' she said. 'She knows it!' Mum picked up her knife and chopped off the stems from the leaves with one angry stroke. 'Bisola, I would appreciate it if you would not bring such things into this house.'

'Grace, why won't you be sensible?' Aunty said. 'You are pregnant and at your most vulnerable. You have to protect yourself.'

Kuki stood in the corridor, out of sight, her fingers kneading her T-shirt. Aunty's voice was quiet as if she was trying to sound soothing and kind, but her words were razor sharp.

'Bisola, you should know by now that I do not believe in these old folk tales about wicked spirits, these Abiku, that haunt families and hurt children. But even if I did, Kuki is almost thirteen now. She is the living proof that we have won and overcome. Nothing will happen to us, to this baby or to Kuki!'

2

MOJI

Kuki counted her steps as she walked to
school. It wasn't far, just a couple of blocks,
but she wanted to know when she reached the
middle of the walk, the point where she was closer
to school than to Dr D's house. She had decided to
start being nervous only from the halfway point.

She hated her new school.

The kids simply ignored her. On her first day,
weeks ago, some of them had been nice. But she
had messed it up by being so nervous that she had
only managed stiff replies that had come out
sounding either unfriendly or stupid. She cringed
at the thought of that first day. Why was she
always so shy in new situations? And why couldn't
her mum have just let them stay in their old flat

close to her old school? She had never been one to have many friends, but at least there she had had Nkechi. Nkechi, who was always drawing things. They had sort of found each other because they'd been the only two to stay in class during break.

Kuki sighed.

Just as she reached the corner where the block of flats stood, an ear-splitting creak of rusty gates had her almost jumping off the sidewalk. A tiny squeal slipped from her lips at the same time as a gasp of recognition from the tall girl who had appeared through the gates.

Kuki recognized her too. Moji, the loud, popular girl in her class.

At first Moji's eyes flitted almost fearfully across the street, as if she wanted to check that Kuki was alone. Then her face tightened into a scowl.

'Hi,' Kuki mumbled awkwardly, and hurried on round the corner. If only she had that very convenient superpower of disappearing into thin air! She was practically invisible in class all day, anyway. She might as well have that superpower!

Now she had forgotten how many steps she

had counted. She would have to recount tomorrow.

'Wait!' Moji's voice called from behind.

Kuki slowed down and peered gingerly over her shoulder. Was she calling her?

Moji caught up with her. 'Do you live around here?'

Kuki nodded. 'Just down the road.'

'How come I've never seen you around?' Moji asked accusingly, as if Kuki had purposely kept information from her.

'I just moved here, remember?'

Moji was silent for a while.

Kuki wondered if she should say something. She thought frantically about what might be an interesting thing to say but as usual when she was nervous, her thoughts went all fuzzy and her lips went numb. Moji was one of those kids who were always surrounded by others. She was always saying something loud or funny. A bit too loud and braggy for Kuki's liking. She had always felt rather afraid of Moji.

'You don't have any friends yet?' Moji said.

'Um . . .' Kuki swallowed. OK, this was embarrassing.

'Just stick with me. I'll hook you up with some friends.'

'Oh . . . ehm, thanks,' Kuki mumbled. Where had that come from? And why did Moji suddenly want to be nice to her? She had never so much as looked at her once in class. But Moji did have a lot of friends. It would be nice to—

'My bag is too heavy,' Moji said, stopping abruptly. She flung her bag to the ground.

Kuki stopped and waited.

'Can you help me?' Moji asked her. She was staring at Kuki now with piercing, questioning eyes. The air around them tensed.

'Help you with what?' Kuki asked.

'To carry my bag, of course!' Moji said, sounding exasperated.

'Oh, ehm, all right . . .' Kuki picked up the bag and swung it over her shoulder along with hers.

'That's so nice of you,' Moji said. Her voice sounded overly sweet now, like overripe cashews. 'So which house do you live in?'

'The light-green one at the very end of the road. Number fourteen,' Kuki said.

Moji nodded. 'So what do you do, afternoons?'

'Oh, nothing much, really . . .'

'You can hang out with us. We are planning to go to the beach one of these days.'

'Oh, that would be—'

'Hey, Tai!' Moji shouted. 'I knew that was your big head the minute I saw it bobbing round the corner.' She crossed the street and joined a group of kids wearing the same blue uniforms as them. Moji bumped fists with the guy who seemed to be Tai and then she hugged one of the girls in the group.

Kuki stopped in her tracks, not knowing what to do. Would Moji come back? Was she supposed to follow her? And just join her in the group?

The kids were almost out of sight before she finally began to trudge slowly after them. Moji's bag on her back was as heavy as her thoughts.

Moji hadn't looked back once.

3

SCHOOL AND OTHER PAINS

School was like one of those nightmares in which you move around in slow motion, trying to get people to listen to you, but everyone just keeps on doing their thing and ignoring you. You have to tell them something really important, it's an emergency even, and you are trying really hard to get them to take you seriously. You are trying to yell at them, but your voice comes out as a whisper. And no one cares anyway . . .

Kuki lowered her head when she saw that the class was almost half full already. She still wasn't sure which was worse: not being noticed at all or being stared at with bored eyes.

She had hoped that not so many kids would be

in class so early, but Moji was already surrounded by her usual group of admirers: Bunmi, Jenny and Faith. As always, she was bragging about something. Kuki slipped past Moji and dropped the bag under her desk as discreetly as possible. But just as she turned to hurry to her seat, she heard a giggle behind her and a snort. Then Joe's loud voice: 'Oh, so Moji, you now have a bag carrier! Wow! Tough babe! Respect!' He strolled through the desks and offered Moji his fist to bump. Moji looked very pleased with herself.

Kuki slipped behind her desk but couldn't help noticing Bunmi and Jenny give her weird looks. At least Faith had only looked away, she thought grimly. Sometimes she felt Faith might be nice if she wasn't always hanging out with Moji! She had smiled at her a couple of times and said hello.

First subject was maths.

Moji let out a frustrated moan when Mrs Chukudi came in. 'The homework was so annoying, I didn't do it,' Kuki heard her whisper.

Kuki was good at maths. Actually, she was good at most subjects, except for sport which she wasn't allowed to do. She was already dreading

PE, the last subject of the day. Her fainting episode when she was little had been during PE The doctor had done some checks and then exempted her from school sports. When she switched to this new school, Kuki had begged her mum to let her join PE class again but she had refused.

'But, Mum, I haven't fainted since I was six!' she had cried. 'I'm fine!'

'I know, Kuki!' Her mum had shrugged. 'But it's doctor's orders! I can't change it.'

But Kuki knew it was because her mum worried about her, as much as she had when she was ill as a tiny baby. She might say she was not superstitious, but maybe she was still thinking about Kuki's name too.

So now, here in this new school, she was once again the weirdo, sitting on a bench and watching others run around and have fun. And the PE teachers always made her sit down and watch. *Even if you don't take part physically, you can still be a part of the team!* Kuki rolled her eyes anytime she heard this. She wasn't part of any team and watching others in a team wasn't going to change that! The worst was when the teacher made her assist. *Bring me the net, Kuki! Throw the ball back into the field, Kuki.* How boring was that!

Today wasn't going to be any different.

'Kuki will be the referee!' Mr Lawal, the sports teacher announced, and Kuki sighed. Being the referee was the worst of all. It only made the other kids mad at her!

Kuki blew the whistle and raised her arm. From the corner of her eye, she suddenly saw something big and round fly towards her. But it was too late to react. Before she could even move, she felt a sharp pain in her head.

There was an outburst of giggling and she saw Moji and her friends whispering among themselves. Obviously, someone had hit her with the basketball on purpose.

'What's going on over there? Back to your positions, children.' Mr Lawal's voice cut through the hall and everyone dispersed quickly. Kuki rubbed her head and tried not to cry.

When it was all over, she hurried out of the hall in relief. At least it was the weekend now, so she was through with school for the week! But that meant Aunty would be coming over again in the evening. She always came on Fridays. Dr D had asked his sister to stay over with them every weekend, to help out more before Mum's baby came.

Kuki sighed, not sure which was worse – school in the week or Aunty on weekends.

Suddenly she heard running steps in the corridor behind her. She glanced back and caught her breath nervously when she saw it was Moji, waving a notebook at her.

Kuki stopped, confused. Had she forgotten her notebook?

'Here,' Moji said, and thrust the notebook into Kuki's hands. 'Can you do my maths homework? I don't like algebra.'

'What?' Kuki asked, shocked.

'I thought you wanted to be friends? I'm a friend in need, you know!'

Kuki held the notebook as if she had been turned to stone – she didn't know what to say or do.

'Aww, perfect!' Moji said, not giving her a

chance to reply. 'But make sure it looks like my handwriting!' she called as she walked away. 'I don't dot my "i"s. I use a heart instead.'

4

THE MUM AND DAUGHTER MOMENTS YOU REALLY DON'T NEED

'Would you like a birthday party, Kuki?' Mum asked.

Kuki was sitting on her bed, loosening her cornrows.

Mum had been hanging around her room for five minutes now, touching her books, folding the clothes that she had already hung neatly over her chair, and fiddling with her curtains. Now Kuki knew why.

She looked up aghast, dropping her hands in her lap. 'Noooh!'

Mum sighed. 'Let me help you with your hair.'

She sat down on Kuki's bed and Kuki slid to the ground in front of her, taking one of her pillows to sit on.

'Kuki, I know you are shy and don't like being the centre of attention, but I think it might really help you to open up to other kids! Inviting some classmates over could be a wonderful way to get to know them better.'

'I already know my classmates very well and I really do not need to get to know them better,' Kuki grumbled.

'We've been here for almost two months now and you have never brought anyone home or gone out to play with anyone.'

'Mum! I don't go out to *play*! I'm not seven any more.'

'You know what I mean, Kuki. Hang out or meet up or whatever you young people say nowadays.'

Kuki rolled her eyes. She couldn't believe this.

'Kuki, you shouldn't always shut yourself in here, away from the world. Let others in! You really are much too shy. It's not good for you to—'

'I am not shutting myself away from anybody! And I can't have a birthday party because I don't have anyone to invite!'

'I don't understand,' Mum said, frowning. 'There must be someone nice in your class! Or someone from the neighbourhood? I know we don't have so many kids your age in the street here, but isn't there a nice-looking girl in the flats at the corner? Have you tried making friends with her? Maybe she even goes to your school? We could invite her?'

'No way!' Kuki cried, her eyes brimming with angry tears. 'I don't want anyone coming here. I don't want a party and I don't even want a birthday! Birthdays are annoying. They are the best reminder of what a loser you are because you are going to be thirteen and you don't even have a single friend to celebrate with!'

Mum stopped loosening her hair and Kuki could feel her eyes on the back of her head, staring at her in shock.

'I'm worried about you, Kuki.'

Kuki turned to face her. 'Mum, I'm fine, really. I'm sorry.'

'Is it because of what Bisola said in the kitchen the other day?'

Kuki stared at her, confused. How come she was talking about Aunty now?

'You really shouldn't let her nonsense talk get to you. You do know we are fine, right? And that nothing will happen to us?' Mum leant forward, her worried eyes searching Kuki's. 'And even if we believed those Abiku myths, they all say that the thirteenth birthday is a milestone. As soon as you are thirteen, you are no more a child and you are out of danger. So either way, myth or no myth, you are fine now, Kuki.' Her belly looked like a tightly blown-up balloon, so delicate, and Kuki felt worse for worrying her.

'Oh, that doesn't bother me at all, Mum. I never believed in such superstitious stories. I mean, wicked spirits living inside of you? Really, Mum!'

'That's my girl,' Mum said and got up. 'Your hair's done.'

She stretched out her arm and pulled Kuki up into a hug. Kuki snuggled into her, surprised at the sudden urge she felt to tighten the hug.

5

RUINED PLANTAINS

'No! You didn't actually tell him that, did you?' Mum said, giggling.

'I did,' Dr D said. 'You should have seen his face. It was hilarious!'

Mum doubled over, almost choking. 'You really are a case, D,' she said, and placed a hand on his arm.

The fact that Mum and Dr D worked in the same hospital meant they were always talking about work and colleagues over dinner. Kuki was bored.

Dr D leant over and offered Mum a slice of plantain on his fork. 'A special one for my baby,' he said with a wink, and Mum ate the plantain with a smile, even though there were lots of plantains on her own plate.

Ugh! They were so embarrassing.

Aunty was sulking. She stared into the spaces between them, chewing her food with very regular bites as if her mouth were a machine.

'How was your day, Kuki?' Dr D asked.

That was his usual and only question, every single day. He and Kuki didn't really have anything to say and it was always rather awkward between them, especially now that they had moved into his house.

'Oh, good, thank you,' Kuki replied. That was her usual and only reply.

He nodded and smiled and looked like he wanted to say something else. But Kuki quickly looked back at her plate and then he didn't.

It was strange that her mum now had a husband but she still didn't have a dad. Kuki had always wondered what it would have been like to have had a dad.

'Why are you always separating your food like that?' Aunty asked sharply, the first time she had spoken over dinner.

Kuki grasped her fork tightly and stared at her

plate. The plantains were on one side, the beans on the other, and Kuki had carefully placed a dollop of stew between them at the top of her plate. She hated it when different foods got all mixed up. The worst was when everything was swimming in stew.

Kuki shrugged.

'What is wrong with this child? Why does she always do such strange things? This child is weird!' Without warning, Aunty leant over and snatched Kuki's fork out of her hand. Then she swept it across the plate.

Kuki stared at her plate in horror. Aunty had mixed everything up. She had slammed the plantains right into the beans and the stew was everywhere.

'What do you think happens to the food you eat in your belly? It all jumbles up to become one big mess!'

'Bisola, leave the child alone,' Dr D said in a low voice.

Kuki could see the anger in Mum's face; she was trying to hold herself back.

'If she is going to be thirteen tomorrow then

24

she should really not be playing around with food like a small child,' Aunty shrugged. She dropped Kuki's fork back into the mess she had made and continued eating her own food.

Kuki swallowed the piece of plantain in her mouth but her appetite was gone.

'Well, no need to look so tragic now. I'm only worried about you acting weird,' Aunty mumbled, looking a little sheepish.

'I am finished,' Kuki said, turning to her mum. 'May I get up?'

'Yes, honey, please do,' Mum said with a smile at Kuki and a murderous glance at Aunty.

6

WHO IS WEIRD?

The next morning while eating her bowl of cornflakes, Kuki was actually almost regretting that she'd refused to have a party.

Her mum had decorated the dining room so nicely, with balloons hanging off the lamp, and colourful paper chains hanging on the wall. She'd placed a pretty tablecloth on the table and strewn little chocolates and sweets all over it. And in the middle of the table she had set up a little pyramid of three colourfully wrapped gifts for her to open later. Kuki had already discovered a really sweet-looking cake with pale-blue icing in the fridge. Her favourite colour. It was almost sad to have all this decoration and cake just for the three of them. She hoped Aunty wouldn't stay to celebrate with them.

She vaguely remembered her mum whispering early that morning, 'Don't oversleep, my love. You don't want to get into trouble for being late on your birthday!' Then a soft kiss on her forehead. 'Happy birthday, ife mi. I have to rush, but Dr D and I will be back early to have cake with you.'

Kuki had placed her empty bowl in the kitchen sink and the milk back on the shelf when she heard the door creak and open slightly. But no one came in.

The silence in the house suddenly seemed very loud.

'Aunty?' she whispered.

There was no reply. Then Kuki saw eyes peering at her through the gap in the door.

'Aunty?' Kuki said, gripping the kitchen table.

'Good morning, Kokumo!' Aunty finally stepped into the room.

Kuki swallowed nervously. What did she want? Was she spying on her?

Feeling uncomfortable, Kuki smoothed her plaits and said, 'I . . . have to go to school.'

'Are you feeling all right?' Aunty asked, half

sitting on the table. She was looking at Kuki so intensely it was as if she expected her to suddenly explode.

Kuki nodded warily.

'Well, then get up and walk around and let us see if it is true!'

'Heh?' Kuki could hardly hide her irritation, but she walked to the door and back. She felt like a goat for sale at the market, being examined for meaty legs and a healthy-looking hide.

'Very good,' Aunty said after a while. 'And you don't feel in any way strange?'

'No!' Kuki said, and shook her head vigorously. 'Why?'

'Do you ever feel like there is someone else inside your head telling you what to do? Making you do strange things?' she asked.

Kuki laughed. She couldn't help it. A snort just slipped out before she could stop it. But when she saw that Aunty wasn't smiling, she yanked her face back into place.

'No!' she replied emphatically. 'Aunty, I am not possessed by an Abiku! I don't even believe in them!'

'But you should!' Aunty cut in. 'You should, Kokumo! Don't joke with the matter. These little mischievous spirits exist. They take over a family and they possess the children.'

Aunty was trying to speak quietly but because she was speaking with such force, her voice came out like a snake hissing. Her hands were on her hips and she bent towards Kuki as she spoke.

Kuki took a small step backwards. She was beginning to feel really uneasy now. Afraid.

'They possess a child at birth and become one with it!' Aunty hissed, her eyes widening dramatically. 'But then these evil little imps get homesick for their spirit world and they begin to visit it. And each time they leave, the child faints and falls ill, but the wicked Abiku do not care. Then one day they go away for ever and the child dies!'

Kuki gulped. Her hands had begun to tremble and she folded them into each other.

'I am not possessed, Aunty. I would know!'

'Then why did your father name you Kokumo? Why did he want to protect you with your name? He must have known! He must have had the same thought!'

Protect her? Her name had always felt more like a curse than a protection.

'I am never ever ill. And today I turned thirteen! I thought those myths say the danger is over at thirteen because you are no longer a child?'

Aunty stared at her for a moment, then nodded. 'Yes, maybe you are one of the lucky ones. But you must be careful, nevertheless. Watch out for anything strange. Don't forget your mother is pregnant. She is vulnerable too. The Abiku like to possess a child around the time of birth.'

She rummaged in the folds of the wrapper tied around her waist and handed Kuki a little package of green flowery paper. 'Happy birthday,' she said, and was gone.

'Oh!' was all Kuki managed to say in her surprise. A gift was the very last thing she had expected. She tore off the wrapping and saw a set of silver earrings. They were pretty silver rings with bells dangling at the bottom. But they were quite large. Nothing like the little studs Kuki would normally wear, and which she hardly ever remembered to put in.

Kuki released her breath, which she had been holding in her chest the whole time. Aunty was so intense and so confusing. She remembered her words the other night. *This child is weird.* Kuki rolled her eyes. If anyone in this house was weird, then it was Aunty, not her.

7

A BIRTHDAY ADVENTURE

Kuki flung her rucksack in the corner of her room as she hummed 'happy birthday to me' in an extra-sad whining tone. The earlier excitement about her birthday had disappeared. It *was* depressing not having a party. She hadn't mentioned her birthday to anyone in school and so it had gone unnoticed all day.

At least she was glad about the quiet in the house. Coming back from school on Mondays was the best because then Aunty was finally gone for the week.

She glanced at the pale-blue cake in the fridge and felt like punching it. Mum and Dr D promising to come back early from work today to celebrate with her was so unnecessary! As if she had asked them to! Why wouldn't they just understand that she didn't need birthdays in her life? Birthdays were fake, exaggerated events that people who weren't important used to make themselves important. She didn't need that. It only drew attention to the fact that she didn't have anyone in her life to be important for.

At least she'd had Nkechi around on her last birthday. Although Mum pretending that having one friend over for your birthday was enough to call it a party had been rather embarrassing. Why did birthdays always have to be so fussy?

She spent the end of the afternoon lazing around but feeling restless. Aunty's weird behaviour had unnerved her. She sat on her bed and tried to fold her legs into the yoga lotus position she'd seen her mum do sometimes. After three tries she yelped in pain and gave up trying to make it perfect. She placed the backs of her hands on her knees and took long, deep breaths. Aunty's words had been ringing in her head all day. *They possess a child and become one with it*. Surely if there was a spirit inside her, she would know? She could feel her heart beating and her breath flowing in and out of her lungs. She even noticed the blood throbbing through her veins. But there was no second heartbeat, no quivering inside her, nothing!

'O spirit inside of me, give me a sign!' Kuki said in a low reverent voice.

'Yes, I am inside of you, Kuki! I, your twin spirit. I possessed your body on the day of your birth and have been one with you ever since!' Kuki replied in a high-pitched voice.

Suddenly there was a sharp pain below her ribs. Then a kind of ripple in her belly. Kuki went absolutely still. And then a low rumbling sound. Her belly was asking for food!

She burst into giggles. Goodness, this was so stupid. She loosened her legs out of the awful position and glanced at the clock. It was almost five! Suddenly the thought of her mum and Dr D coming back and all the birthday fussing made her heart skip a beat and double its pace. She jumped up, grabbed a handful of chin-chin from the kitchen and fled the house.

Outside, she looked up and down the street as

she munched. She definitely didn't feel like bumping into Moji now. But even though the street was empty, on a weird impulse, she turned left.

Dr D's house was at the end of the street and at the edge of their housing estate. A little path led through some tall elephant grass and trees, into the hinterland of Lekki. When Dr D had driven Kuki and her mum to his house with their belongings squeezed into cartons and boxes, it had felt like they were driving for ever, to the very edge of the African continent even. They had left the mainland behind them, crossed the lagoon over the never-ending bridge, and Kuki had stared at the daunting skylines of Victoria Island and the Lekki peninsula in front of them with fear. She had crossed over for a beach outing with her mum before, but on that day of their move her belly had bobbed up and down like the houses on stilts in the lagoon below. Dr D had talked all the way, obviously trying to make Kuki, who had not said a word, excited about Lekki. But Lekki had seemed so far. She had felt uprooted. As if every single last connection to her past life had been ripped out of her on that day.

Kuki had never felt any interest in investigating Lekki up till now. She was surprised at her firm, determined steps as she strutted down the path. She felt light-headed and relieved to have left the house. Why had she never gone this way before? She knew that Dr D and Mum strolled here sometimes in the evenings. The path went past the tall wall of the neighbouring housing estates. Kuki heard children's voices in the distance. They sounded happy. She tried to ignore them.

After a while the sides of the path became bushier. The children's voices thinned out and were replaced by the twittering of birds. It was beautiful out here and she soaked up the quieter sounds of nature. The buzz of busy insects, the wind whistling between the leaves and stalks of bushes, and a distant swishing sound. The sound of waves? She had to be getting closer to the ocean.

The bushes and grasses stood in swampy puddles. The path had also become soggy and she wondered if it was safe to continue. But now she wanted to see where the path led. Someone had obviously created it or at least had trodden it down over time. She looked up at the sky, which was beginning to grey, and wished she had brought her phone or thought to wear her watch. She had actually left her phone at home on purpose because she hadn't felt like talking to anyone. But now, she would have to hurry if she wanted to make it back before dark. Mum's golden rule was: *Go where you like, see who you want but be back by dusk!* Not that she had ever needed the rule. Even at their former flat, Kuki had hardly ever gone out. Her only friend had lived far away, so they had only talked in school.

The path cut through trees into a little forest. There was still just enough light to see it. Another strange impulse led her forward, and she jogged on. The twittering of birds became louder and the air cooler.

Then, very abruptly, the forest ended and the path split into two. The more used-looking path seemed to head back towards the town. The second path was so overgrown it was hardly recognizable. She hesitated briefly but then with an uncanny flutter of excitement in her belly, she took the overgrown path, which went in and out of the trees. When it turned a sharp corner she gasped in surprise.

She was standing in front of rusty gates, overgrown with climbing plants, the tallest gates she had ever seen. As her eyes adjusted to what lay beyond, they almost fell out of her head.

A wide driveway lined with majestic palm trees curved all the way to a huge mansion. On either side of the entrance was a series of massive pillars and tall statues. But everything looked abandoned. What was this place? The pillars were peeling, the driveway overgrown with weeds, and the faded facade of pale stone was disintegrating. Who had built such a villa and then abandoned it? And yet it was an enchanting sight. She might as well have discovered a lost part of the great walls of Benin.

She stared at the mansion, wishing she could get a closer look. Just then she noticed a bar missing, and a space in the gate large enough for a person to . . .

Without thinking, she squeezed through.

8

THE HOUSE OF SHELLS

As soon as her foot touched the driveway, Kuki felt a rush of cool breeze on her skin. Goosebumps climbed up her arms and she felt more excited than she had been in a very long time. This was like a fairy-tale adventure. And just an evening walk away from home, school and her annoying life!

She walked slowly, taking in all the details. The mix of extravagance, crumbling beauty, giant palm trees and rustling bushes felt like a dream. In the distance, Kuki heard the sound of waves crashing, like the background music of a movie, gently building up the atmosphere of a scene. The ocean had to be somewhere just beyond the house.

Bright specks of whiteness, scattered between the gravel and weeds of the driveway, caught her eye. She bent down and picked one up. A cowrie. Shells and parts of shells, in different colours and shades, were everywhere. She glimpsed fan-shaped shells in faded orange and little spiral shells with tints of light purple as she approached the house.

At the entrance the statues of two female dancers were so tall that Kuki only reached up to their knees. Their fingers and noses had broken off and their sculpted clothes had crumbled. A large conch – brown-and-white checked on the outside and pink inside – lay on the ground by the front door, as if to invite her in. Kuki picked it up and held it to her ear, listening to the sound of the ocean inside. She had never seen one this large. It was as big as the giant snails they sold in huge baskets at the market. Kuki always felt like helping the giant snails escape when she saw them crawl up the sides of the baskets.

The door was massive and, once upon a time, intricately carved. Now the wood was almost grey from wind and weather and a soft layer of red dust had filled in the details, but it was still beautiful.

Kuki traced a finger along spiralling patterns that could have been flowers, shells or curled-up chameleon tails.

She put down the conch and pushed the door. It opened with a loud, splintery creak. She flinched at the sound, wondering if she was being too bold. After all, this was private property and she was trespassing. But from what she could see, the inside looked just as abandoned and forlorn and beautiful as the outside. In a hallway of past grandeur, a large chandelier wrapped in the scraps of a mouldy protection cloth dangled from a crumbling ornate ceiling.

Kuki stepped in. The air was heavy and humid inside and tinged with a musty smell.

She walked up the broad winding staircase that was the centrepiece of the grand hallway. The railing was covered with thick dust, so she avoided touching it. Upstairs she tiptoed from one room to another, hoping to discover more signs of the past owners. There wasn't much left, no pictures on the walls, though she could see the lighter rectangular spots on the walls, where large paintings had once hung. Old shelves with elaborate carved details were now empty and covered with cobwebs. Had the owners planned to come back for these? Why had they bothered to wrap the chandeliers and empty the shelves? For some reason they had never returned.

A large four-poster bed stood right in the middle of the last bedroom, framed by the remains of old curtains. The greying wisps of cloth shrouded the bed like long, ghostly fingers. Suddenly a gust of wind whizzed in through the broken window, making the dangling shreds of cloth tremble. A shadow fell across the curtains as the dull light outside changed and faded. It was growing dark. A weird, scary thought crossed Kuki's mind. What if someone was lying in the bed? Her heart began to race. She wanted to tiptoe backwards but strangely found herself moving forward. She wanted to know.

But the bed was empty, except for piles of shells. It was as if someone had been playing with them, separating them into heaps of different shapes and sizes. There were more cowries, two large white conches and many colourful periwinkle shells. And scattered in between was sand.

Kuki hurried back downstairs. It was almost totally dark now. One last look around the rest of the house and she would have to go home. She didn't want to leave yet.

She discovered an elegant large room, like a ballroom out of a fairy tale, with the largest mirrors she had ever seen. Two sides of the room were mirrored; at the other end were floor-to-ceiling windows that faced overgrown bushes outside. Shells were strewn around the floor. She imagined lively owambe parties, women with tall geles on their heads and men in sweeping agbadas dancing to pulsating music, and bobbing trays filled with soft yam-swallow, party-jollof and fried meat. Why had this beautiful place been abandoned?

She traced her finger along the cold mirrors. Some were stained by dark spots around the edges or blurring with age. Kuki stumbled over a pile of shells that she had not noticed, scattering them around the room. Her sudden movement was reflected in all the mirrors around her, as if a crowd had suddenly appeared. Nervously she ran from the room and through a corridor towards a door that stood ajar and seemed to lead outside, to the back of the house. Kuki wondered that animals didn't live in here if the doors stood open like this. She shuddered as she imagined rats and lizards and even snakes creeping through the dark crevices of the house.

Her eyes widened as she stepped outside on to a large terrace. A majestic tree stood in the centre of a beautifully designed mosaic circle. The tiles were a faded blue and arranged in swirling patterns. The tree was strangely formed, its branches like twisted arms and fingers stretched out as if in agony against the greying sky. Its thick, whitish-grey trunk was gnarled, and its leaves gleamed like dark emeralds in the fading light. All other thoughts faded away into the shadows of this tree. Kuki stood unmoving, as if turned to stone, trapped in the moment like the statues in front of the house. She felt strangely overwhelmed by its beauty.

A sudden movement behind the tree trunk caught her attention.

Was that a shadow? A . . . a hand?

She gasped and felt her legs weaken in shock. Why had she thought to break in? Someone lived here. She was probably in really big trouble.

Kuki took a careful step backwards but it was too late. The hand grew into an arm and the arm into a person. A thin wisp of a girl stepped out of the shadow of the tree.

'It is a fine place here, isn't it?' she said in a whispery voice.

She was about Kuki's age. Her eyes were large and stood out in her angular face. They were the only soft things about her. She was all elbows and knees and edges. Her hair was plaited in rough-looking all-back cornrows and her ears stuck out slightly. A cowrie shell hung on a leather band at her throat.

'Yes,' Kuki replied. She had worried for nothing. This girl was definitely not the owner of this estate. Her dress was worn and a little too short. She looked like a street kid. And this was probably her hideout.

'I love to watch the sun end its journey,' the strange girl said. She patted the silvery trunk. 'With my back against the tree and the sun climbing down to rest after its hard day, I always feel like the world is at my feet.' She looked at Kuki with a sly glint in her eyes. 'Do you want to see?'

Kuki glanced beyond the tree and the bushes and saw the setting sun, orange against a purple sky, and the magnificent dark-shimmering Atlantic.

In that moment the last bit of the sun slipped into the ocean and the purple sky lost its glow.

Kuki's eyes widened in fear at the same time as the girl's. It was dark. She was late!

Kuki was edging back towards the house when the tree suddenly lit up with red dots of light. Fireflies. It was an eerie, mesmerising sight, but Kuki had no time left. She turned her back on the strange girl and ran from the house.

9

NIGHT NOISES AND SHADOWS

The evening wind gathered strength and swept through the Lekki hinterland, scattering branches and leaves around the path. Kuki huffed and puffed her way through the first stretch of forest, frightened by the wind's cold breath on the back of her neck and the strange rustling sounds carried with it. Almost like murmuring voices. A branch suddenly cracked and fell on the path right in front of her. She yelped, jumped over it and began to run even faster.

The fireflies she had seen in the weird tree earlier now appeared in the forest too, giving it a reddish, eerie glow. Was she imagining it or did that swishing noise in the leaves above sound like laughter? Why did it feel like the fireflies were coming closer?

When Kuki got to the crossroads she paused to catch her breath. To her dismay, the last stretch of forest was now pitch dark. Goosebumps marched down her back like a thousand soldier ants. Now she really wished she had brought her phone for its torch.

She looked back fearfully. The fireflies that had seemed to be following her had disappeared. But the darkness ahead seemed just as daunting. Still gasping for breath, she felt her throat constrict and her eyes begin to burn with hot tears. There was no way she could go in there!

Suddenly there was a crackling sound behind her. Footsteps!

Her heart began hammering against her chest and she looked around desperately for a spot to hide.

'It is quite dark, isn't it?' a whispery voice said.

Kuki jumped high into the air, as if she had just stepped on a bush of devil beans. It was the girl from the house of shells.

'I thought you might want some company on

your way back,' she said.

Kuki almost cried out with relief. 'Yes!' she managed. 'Yes, please, that would be really nice.'

Kuki followed the girl's shadow as she headed into the forest. It was alive with croaking and bristling noises. The world of nocturnal animals had fully awoken. Kuki trod as lightly as she could, fearing to draw attention to herself. The girl was so slim and nimble that she hardly made any noise at all. Something flew past, so low and so quickly that Kuki ducked her head, letting out a strangled cry.

'Bats,' the girl whispered. 'They are not dangerous. They are just searching for water to drink after waking up from a hot, dry day's sleep.'

But nevertheless, Kuki noticed the girl walked faster and she did the same. Soon after, the path ahead brightened. The street lights from the estates lit up the sky and she could see the path clearly now. They had made it! She gasped with relief and they ran the last steps.

'That was creepy!' Kuki panted. 'Thanks for taking me.'

The girl simply nodded, her large soft eyes

flickering nervously about her.

'But what about you?' Kuki asked. 'How will you get home?'

The girl shrugged. 'I don't mind the dark and I am used to being alone.'

'What's your name? I'm Kuki.'

The girl didn't reply immediately. She regarded Kuki closely, as if contemplating whether she could trust her.

'Enilo,' she said finally.

'Enilo . . .' Kuki repeated slowly. 'Oh, that's a name I have never heard before—'

'That is my name!' the girl interrupted with a vehemence that stunned Kuki. She looked at the girl in surprise and saw fear in her large eyes.

Kuki felt sorry for her. Had she run away from home? Was she hiding from someone? She looked so skinny, like she could do with a big plate of food.

Kuki glanced anxiously at the brightly lit windows of Dr D's house.

'You shouldn't really be out in the dark like this,' Enilo said quietly. 'Not today.' She glanced over her shoulder at the gloomy forest.

Kuki looked at her, surprised.

'And the house of shells is not the best place to be at night.'

Dr D's front door opened and a ray of light streamed out into the front yard.

'Isn't that the same for you?' Kuki replied, turning towards the house.

But there was no reply from Enilo. Kuki turned back, searching the shadows, but Enilo had disappeared. Like a quiet, stealthy creature into the dark crevice of its shell.

10

LATE BIRTHDAY
BATTLES

'You're lucky it's your birthday, Kuki, and that we're not going to scold you today,' Mum said with a sharp, arched eyebrow.

She didn't look happy at all and Kuki immediately felt terribly guilty.

'I'm so sorry, Mum. I totally forgot the time.'

'But you knew we had planned to come home early, to spend the evening with you!'

Kuki stared at Mum's feet in her yellow flip-flops, tapping on the floor, and felt like the worst spoilsport of all time.

'You could at least have taken your phone with—'

Dr D appeared behind Mum. 'There's our

birthday girl, finally!' he called, interrupting Mum and clapping his hands cheerfully. 'Grace, I made you a cup of tea and it's getting cold.' He pulled Kuki's mum gently into the house and winked at Kuki.

Kuki let out a relieved breath, grateful for Dr D's intervention.

Dr D and Mum had already set the table, and the cake and a big bowl of puff-puffs sat in the middle looking lovely. Kuki realized how hungry she was.

'Girls, I'll be right there with you in a minute! I just had a great idea, but I need to go and dig around in some old boxes first.'

Mum shook her head. 'What is he up to now? I thought we could finally have cake. I'm starving. This man, ehn!'

'Mum, the cake is wonderful. I love it,' Kuki said. 'And thank you for all the decorations. It was a nice surprise this morning.'

'I wanted you to feel special, Kuki. You know you are my special number one person, right?' She put a finger to her lips and winked. 'Come here, hon!' She drew Kuki into a tight hug.

Dr D came in just at that moment. 'Oh, that's how I love to see my girls. Hugging and smiling.'

Mum broke into a wide grin and Kuki also found herself grinning sheepishly.

'But I have to warn you. The smiles will turn to cries of disappointment and frustration in a few minutes.' He threw a battered box on the table. It was so old that half of the contents slid out, releasing a cloud of dust, making Mum sneeze. It was an almost unrecognizable game of Monopoly.

'You are facing the greatest Monopoly champion of all time in the good old university days in Zaria. We used to play Monopoly every night in the hostel!'

'Good grief, D, what is this?' Mum cried and held up some old bits of Monopoly money. 'This looks like a rat nibbled at it! And why is everything in the box so brown?'

Kuki giggled and picked up the 'Go to jail' chance card, which was so faded she could hardly read it.

'Do not say anything against my dear Monopoly friend here! I went to university in the north. Do you know how dusty it is up there in the harmattan season? Half the Sahara drifted into our hostel rooms and covered our clothes and books overnight. Every year in harmattan season, everything we owned turned red!'

Kuki grinned at Dr D's proud expression. The game was an absolute wreck.

'You are all just afraid to lose.'

'OK, that's it!' Mum said. 'Kuki, let's show him what we are made of!'

'I'm in!' Kuki said and gave her mum a high five.

'As long as I'm allowed to disinfect my hands before Dr D passes me the trophy for beating him hands down!' Mum whispered loudly in Kuki's ear.

Dr D feigned shock and Mum chortled while Kuki began to eagerly separate the cards into the right piles. The evening looked like it was going to be fun after all.

11

FRIENDS YOU DON'T WANT TO HAVE

Kuki crouched close to the hedge in front of Moji's block of flats.

How annoying that there was no other way to get to school. She had left for school extra early today to avoid meeting her. She definitely wasn't going to become Moji's school assistant! Which seemed to be Moji's plan for her.

Moji had called her to join her group during break the previous day. But then she had pushed money into Kuki's hand and asked her to 'be a friend' and buy her a sandwich at the kiosk. And the money hadn't even been enough. Kuki had paid the difference with her own lunch money. And when she had returned with the sandwich,

Moji had taken it with a big, fake smile like she had taken the maths homework she had done for her as well, and then ignored her. Kuki had felt so stupid standing there. She had wondered if there was something wrong with her. Was she meant to just join in and make comments on the things they were saying? Shouldn't they have at least opened up their circle for her to join them and stand among them? She had felt so awkward staring at their backs, feeling like an impostor, and after a while had slipped away unnoticed.

Krack! The sound of a window creaking open somewhere had her ducking her head even further below the hedge.

She sighed, feeling foolish, and darted forward, past the gate, crouching as she moved.

Suddenly she heard steps behind her. Oh no! She straightened out of her embarrassing position and lurched around the corner.

'Phew!' She let out a sigh of relief but immediately staggered back when she saw a tall figure leaning against a tree.

'So early to school?' Moji asked, tilting her head. She was taller than most of the kids in their class, Kuki had found out, because she was older. She had repeated a year.

Moji's arms were folded across her chest and her eyes burnt into Kuki's, making her feel even smaller.

'Oh, ehm . . . yes. My mum said to, ehm . . . to go earlier, yes, because, so there's no risk of being late.'

'So much earlier, ehn?' Moji didn't seem to believe a word.

Kuki nodded, trying to look convincing.

'Nice shoes,' Moji said, abruptly changing the subject. 'Let me try them on.'

Kuki stared at her confused. 'My shoes?'

Moji didn't reply. She just stared at Kuki as if daring her to resist.

No harm in trying on each other's shoes, Kuki thought. She took off one of her trainers. They were her birthday gift from Mum and Dr D. Her new favourites. White with pink stripes. She handed the shoe to Moji, feeling her belly tighten.

Moji took off her sandal and tried to force her foot into the shoe. It didn't fit. Kuki thought of Cinderella's mean stepsisters and had to hide a wicked grin.

'Wouldn't it have been so lovely to exchange shoes for a day? Like friends!' Moji said in a super-sweet voice as she slipped her foot back into her sandal.

Kuki nodded slowly, liking the word 'friends' but not wanting to connect it with Moji.

It was difficult trying to avoid someone who was in your class and lived on your street. Moji was everywhere! And she was bossy and loud and tall. And intimidating. Kuki realized she was now truly scared of her.

When the final school bell rang, she was one of the first to rush through the gate. As she left the building behind, Kuki's mind relaxed and unravel-led and began to push away thoughts of Moji and of school. Instead a feeling of excitement began to take over and bounced around like a rubber ball in her belly. All she could think of was her discovery of the day before. The beautiful house with all those colourful shells strewn about and the strange girl, Enilo.

But at the same time, something gnawed at the bouncing feeling of excitement. A warning. There had definitely been something mysterious about Enilo. Why had she gotten the feeling that the girl lived there? That she was a homeless kid? Kuki remembered her rather shabby appearance. Like the street kids who begged for money in traffic jams and slept under the bridges at night, grouping together for safety. Kuki shook off her worries. She definitely wasn't going to be a snob. Just because someone wasn't well off was not a reason to shun them or imagine things about them. Enilo was about her age, and at that age nobody lived alone in a run-down building.

Back in her bedroom, she slipped out of her uniform and into comfortable shorts and a T-shirt, and hurried through her homework. Then she carefully copied her answers into Moji's exercise book, ignoring the nervous knot in her throat. She was just helping a classmate, that was all. Wasn't that a nice thing to do? Only it seemed to be becoming a regular thing.

It was a huge relief when she finished and pushed Moji's book into her school bag along with her own books. Kuki went into the kitchen to have some leftover cake and puff-puff from her birthday. She poured a dollop of honey on to a plate and before each bite of the soft puff-puff she dipped it into the honey. She glanced out of the window as she munched and realized that her thoughts were straying to the house of shells again. So she looked around the kitchen instead, at the clock, at the ceiling light, and drummed her fingers on the tabletop. The kitchen was silent except for the noises she made and the clock ticking in slow motion.

No! There was no way she was going to spend the afternoon bored at home when she could go out and have an adventure.

She swallowed at the thought of that dark stretch of forest. It had been scary. *But that was only because it was dark.* She had clearly imagined those sounds. It had been just the wind, swishing through the trees, and the fireflies and other night insects and animals waking up.

Kuki glanced up at the clock one last time – her mind was made up.

She quickly washed up her plate and fork, then

grabbed her phone and torch. This time she would be prepared and she would make sure to come back on time. She'd been lucky not to get into trouble the night before.

When she reached the trees, she filled her lungs and ran all the way through, keeping her torch on even though it wasn't dark. Everything seemed normal. Birds chirped and the wind swayed the leaves at the very tops of the trees. There were no bats and no scary whispers, no fireflies, no swishing sounds that echoed like laughter.

The house of shells truly was an amazing sight! Serene and absolutely unexpected in the middle of nowhere. She hurried towards it with eager steps, excited and hoping Enilo would be there. She had been nice to her, had helped her – unlike Moji.

This time she didn't run upstairs but went straight through the mirror room. The back door stood open like the day before and she could already see the blue mosaic tiles reflecting the sun. It almost looked like the door led to a blue ocean. She caught her breath and walked through. The tree was as eerie as ever with its twisted arms and gnarled silver trunk filling the entire courtyard with its presence.

'Enilo?' Kuki whispered, already feeling her heart falling. The girl was nowhere in sight.

But then, a rustling, a thin elbow, and Enilo's large eyes appeared from behind the massive trunk. Kuki felt her belly leap with excitement. She edged forward slowly across the blue mosaic tiles and smiled nervously.

To her surprise Enilo's face disappeared behind the tree. Kuki waited.

'I . . . thought I'd come over again,' she said at last, her voice and her eagerness faltering. When there was no reply she continued, 'I thought we could . . . hang out.' A strange urge came over her and she felt bold. She said something she had never dared to say to anyone before. 'I thought we could be friends?'

'You should not have come!' Enilo's voice drifted towards her, a delicate whisper on the wind. But it might as well have been a slap.

'Oh . . .' was all Kuki managed to say.

'I do not think that being friends is a good idea.'

'Why? I don't understand.'

'You do not want a friend like me!' Enilo's face reappeared. She looked rueful, but her words were not. 'You should go.'

12

THINGS FRIENDS DO

Tears wet her cheeks as Kuki ran along the path to the forest. Embarrassed and frustrated, she fumbled with the torch but it wouldn't go on. She hissed angrily as she hit the torch against her palm.

'Wait!' Enilo's light voice called.

Kuki turned reluctantly, still bristling.

'I am sorry . . . for being mean,' Enilo said. It seemed a very hard thing for her to say.

Kuki went back to rattling the torch and used the distraction to wipe her eyes. 'It was just a suggestion, you know. No problem, if you're not interested. I . . . I have enough friends already, it's not like I really need more friends anyway—'

'I am not used to having . . . friends,' Enilo interrupted.

Kuki nodded slowly. 'Me neither, to be honest.'

'Having friends is not always an easy matter,' Enilo replied. Her large eyes were serious and she spoke slowly, as if she wasn't used to it or as if she liked to think about each word before saying it.

'So what now?' Kuki asked warily.

'I could stroll back with you? Like yesterday?'

Kuki shrugged and they walked into the little forest together. Her torch had finally switched itself back on and she shone it around even though it was really not dark at all. The trees cast only faint shadows, blocking direct sunlight.

'Do you not see clearly when it's getting dark?'

'You mean like night blindness?'

'Yes. Although this is night blindness during the day.'

Kuki couldn't help grinning. 'The torchlight just makes me feel safer, I guess.'

'That is funny,' Enilo said.

'I know, I am weird at times.'

'Me too.'

Enilo padded silently beside her. Kuki noticed

she was barefoot. Then her bare feet came to a halt and Kuki realized they had reached the end of the path.

'What should we do now?' she asked, not wanting to sound too eager again. She would have loved to spend more time with Enilo. It was strange, but in her presence she didn't feel awkward like she usually felt around the kids in school. Maybe it was the slow way she spoke in that whispery voice. Kuki felt very comfortable with her. She had lots of ideas of things they could do. Things she had so often wished she could do with someone. Things that friends do.

Enilo peeked round the bushes towards Dr D's house. She looked very nervous. 'I think I will go back,' she said eventually.

'You could come in?' Kuki said at the same time.

Enilo glanced at her. Now she looked frightened.

'We could have some juice? It's so hot and I am parched.'

'Is anyone home?' Enilo asked. But she was moving back towards the forest. She didn't look happy.

'I don't think so.' Kuki took out her phone from her back pocket and glanced at the time. 'No one will be in for at least an hour.'

Laughter and voices came from behind the walls of the neighbouring estate. Enilo jerked around. At the same time a car turned into the street from the other direction and was driving towards them, tyres crunching. Enilo's eyes flickered from the path behind her to the car in front with a sudden panicked look, then she turned to Kuki and nodded quickly.

Kuki smiled, surprised and happy that Enilo had changed her mind.

'That's just a neighbour in the car,' Kuki said reassuringly as they hurried to the gate. She had a feeling Enilo didn't like being among people.

13

FLUTTERING CURTAINS

Enilo was like a bird trapped in a cage from the moment they stepped into Dr D's house. She looked around with nervous jerks of her head, cocking her head as if she was listening. She hurried to the window to look out and then turned to face Kuki, kneading her fingers.

'Let's go to my room,' Kuki said gently. 'We'll be more comfortable there.'

Kuki closed the door of her bedroom behind them and stayed at the door, watching her.

Enilo glanced at the huge desk. It was Dr D's old desk that took up almost half of the room. She passed Dr D's old black leather chair and walked to Kuki's bookshelf. Kuki suddenly felt a little self-conscious about her room. It was the first time she was having someone over.

'I know it looks a bit like an office,' she said. 'We just moved in, so . . .'

'It's nice to have your very own place, you know,' Enilo said, not looking at her. She pulled out her shell necklace from beneath the neckline of her dress and began to fiddle with it. Kuki felt her cheeks flush. Here she was going on about her room not being perfect and Enilo probably didn't even have a home to call her own.

Enilo trailed her hand along Kuki's books, as if she was beginning to feel more at ease. Her finger stopped at the most tattered one and she pulled it out. She stroked the cover slowly, caressing the worn edges.

'That's my favourite book,' Kuki said, feeling nervous. 'I think I must have read it twenty or thirty times at least. When I like a book I read it over and over again. It makes me feel good. It's like going to visit your favourite place or spending time with your favourite people.' She glanced at Enilo, hoping she wouldn't find her weird.

But Enilo just shrugged. 'I love this book as well.'

'Oh, you've read it?' Kuki said, then immediately felt guilty. She had sounded too surprised that Enilo read books.

Enilo nodded. 'I have read most of these,' she said, then turned and abruptly shoved the book back on to the shelf. She looked so awkward, all bones and edges with her slightly-too-short dress. She placed one foot on the other, then switched feet.

'I'll get us some juice, OK?'

Enilo shrugged again and sat down on Kuki's bed. Kuki hurried to the kitchen.

'So what do you feel like doing?' Kuki said when she came back. She put the tray with glasses and some biscuits on her desk. 'We could play a game, or go to the living room and watch TV or play a computer game.'

Enilo shook her head fiercely.

'OK,' Kuki said reassuringly, 'we can stay in my room and play a game here. Let me see.' She walked to her shelf. 'I have Scrabble and UNO and Dr D has Monopoly, though it's really old and—'

'What was that?' Enilo said suddenly.

Kuki looked up.

71

'There was a clicking sound, like keys. I think someone came in!'

'Oh yes, I heard it, it's probably my mum. She sometimes comes back earlier when traffic is not too bad . . . but it's OK, Enilo, really!'

Enilo was shaking her head wildly. She jumped up and rushed to the window, staring out frantically.

'There is a blue car,' she hissed.

'Oh yes, that's my mum's car. She is very nice,' Kuki whispered. 'And she would be happy to know I have a friend over.'

Enilo shook her head again, gripping the window bars.

'Kuki! I'm home!' her mum's voice called.

Enilo went rigid.

Kuki hurried out of her room. 'Welcome back, Mum!' she called. 'I'll be right there!'

Then she went back into her room, closed the door and leant against it. 'Look, Enilo—' she began, then stopped in surprise.

Her room was empty. Enilo was gone.

The only proof that she had been there was the open window and the fluttering curtain.

14

FAITH

Gbagam! Gbagam!

The final school bell of the week! Everyone rushed out of class as if a three-headed Egungun monster had appeared and started breathing fire.

Kuki picked up her rucksack slowly and began putting her books into her bag. She wasn't feeling too excited. The ordeal of school was over for another week, but a boring weekend lay ahead in which she would do her best to remain in her room and out of the way. But what bothered her the most was that Enilo had not returned.

She sighed. The short time she had spent with Enilo in her room had made her feel elated. She had been so excited at the thought of finally having a friend. But two days had passed and she hadn't returned. And Kuki didn't feel sure about going back to the abandoned house to look for her, in case she was faced with another unfriendly welcome. Enilo obviously had problems. She was extremely shy, to the point of panic, she didn't trust people, and she seemed to be homeless.

'Is it true that you now do Moji's homework for her?'

Kuki jumped, her pencil falling and rolling out of sight underneath the desks. She had thought she was alone in the classroom.

Faith was at the door, staring at her.

Kuki bent down and searched for the pencil, not wanting to reply. But when she got up with the pencil in her hand, Faith was still standing there, waiting for an answer.

Kuki shrugged, grabbed her bag and walked slowly to the door. Was Faith making fun of her? Her belly tightened and her heart began to beat faster when she saw Faith was holding a book in her hand.

'I'm not . . . I can't do your homework as well . . .' she said. 'I'm sorry,' she added through clenched teeth.

Faith looked at her in shock, her eyes widening. 'You actually think I would ask you to do that?'

Kuki stopped in mid-stride, feeling uncertain.

'I am not like Moji!' Faith went on. 'I don't . . . I don't think she's nice to you, sending you around to get things for her and all that.' She was whispering now.

Kuki looked at her in surprise.

'She can be so bossy, don't you think?' Faith stepped into the classroom, glancing behind her.

Kuki didn't know what to say. Was Faith actually trying to take her side? Her heart quickened.

'But you are her friend!' she said, frowning.

Faith swallowed and smiled weakly. 'I—' she started but was cut short.

'Faith!' Moji's tall frame appeared in the doorway. 'What are you still doing here? We have been waiting for you!' Her eyes narrowed. 'Why are you talking to Kuki? What were you discussing?'

Faith took a step back, suddenly looking very small beside Moji. 'I was just getting my notebook,' she said quickly, holding it up. 'Let's go,' she added, trying to edge past.

Moji didn't budge. 'Yes, but what were you talking about? I saw you both whispering.'

'Oh, erm . . . can you imagine! Kuki was just asking me if I wanted to hang out with her!' Faith laughed – a shrill, nasty laugh that vibrated all the way through to Kuki's core.

What? The word screamed inside Kuki's head, but she was so stunned that she couldn't even say it out loud. She just stared at Faith in disbelief. But Faith was avoiding her eyes.

Moji turned to Kuki. 'For real? Are you trying to steal my friends from me, behind my back?' Her voice was low and she took a step towards Kuki. They were now so close that Kuki could smell her deodorant mixed with sweat.

Kuki shook her head. 'No, I wouldn't do that,' she stammered and swallowed. 'I didn't ask . . .' She tried to speak but her voice was squeaky and nothing more would come out.

Faith gave her a panicked look and then grabbed Moji's hand. 'Come on, Moji, let's go,' she said. 'I thought you said the others were waiting. Abeg, let's not waste our time with this one!'

15

AN ABSOLUTE PUZZLE

Kuki slammed the front door as hard as she could. She marched angrily through the house and when she got to her room she kicked the door open and flung her rucksack at the wall. It was only when the bag left her hand that she noticed the slim figure sitting on her bed.

They both yelped at the same time. Then stared at each other in shock.

Then Kuki burst out laughing and Enilo's face softened into a sly grin.

Kuki fell on to her bed beside Enilo and carried on giggling like a cackling hen. She was surprised at herself. But she suddenly felt so elated after her horrible day at school.

Enilo watched her with her confused half-grin. 'What was that about? The way you stormed in like a fury was terrifying!'

Kuki took a deep breath and shook her head. 'School was a pain today but I'm fine now. I'm glad you came.' She glanced at Enilo, then frowned and stared at her open window.

Enilo raised an eyebrow sheepishly. 'I hope it was OK to just come in? I didn't touch anything or go anywhere in the house. I swear! I just sat here waiting.'

'Oh, that's no problem, I was just wondering how you managed to squeeze in through the bars. You are so agile! I couldn't do it.'

Enilo shrugged. 'I am used to hiding and small places . . .' She stopped and there was an awkward silence. 'Anyway, so what about all those games you wanted to play?'

Enilo was so good at Scrabble that Kuki had a hard time keeping up. Enilo won all three rounds.

Kuki stared at her in surprise. She was an absolute puzzle! How come she was so smart if she was homeless and didn't go to school? Or did she?

'What school do you go to?' Kuki asked, while Enilo's hand searched the bag of letter tiles.

But Enilo didn't answer the question. 'Oh no, not another "E",' was all she said instead.

But Kuki saw how tightly Enilo gripped the bag.

Kuki decided to leave it for now. She definitely didn't want to scare off her new friend with questions she wasn't ready to answer. A friend with secrets was still a hundred times better than no friend at all.

16

A SURPRISING
CHANGE OF COLOUR

'Pastel or bright colours?' Kuki called.

'Bright!' she and Enilo said in unison.

'Puff-puff or chin-chin?'

'Puff-puff,' they both said at the same time again.

Kuki scrolled further through her phone and read the next choices.

'Happy end or cliff-hanger?'

'Cliff-hanger, of course!' they yelled.

Enilo's eyes sparkled with excitement and Kuki knew hers looked exactly the same. The afternoon had been so much fun. They lay on her bed facing the ceiling, feet dangling to the floor. They had chosen the same answers for almost all questions.

She had never felt so close and so comfortable with anyone before. They were so alike in so many ways.

'Do you realize we are like—'

'—two halves of a clam shell?' Enilo finished for her.

Kuki grinned. 'That's it! Ha! And that fits perfectly to the next question. Pool or beach?'

'Beach, of course!' Enilo giggled at their perfectly harmonious reply.

'Well, that's not so surprising,' Kuki said. 'We are Lekki kids, after all. We practically live on the beach.'

Kuki thought of her excitement when Dr D had taken them to the beach. How surprised she and her mum had been that they could actually stroll there on foot. She remembered the waves caressing the sand softly that evening, Mum and Dr D walking hand in hand along the beach, shoes dangling in their free hands. The moment had felt so special that she had even stopped worrying how her first day of school the next day would be. Seeing her mum so happy had made her feel hopeful and safe.

Kuki glanced at Enilo. Her face had taken on a faraway thoughtful look. Kuki bit her lip. She had pictured Enilo in the house of shells so often that she now just assumed she lived there. But obviously that couldn't be her home! Was Enilo thinking of her real home? Her parents?

'Gold or silver?' Enilo asked, quickly reading out the next choice. But she was frowning.

'Gold!' Kuki called. 'Definitely gold and lots of it!'

'I don't like gold *or* silver,' Enilo said, frowning even more. Her thin shoulders almost seemed to shudder.

'Oh,' Kuki said. 'Well, never mind. Next question then,' she added quickly, sensing that the mood had suddenly changed. 'Oz or Wonderland?'

But Enilo jumped up and walked to the window.

Kuki sighed and sat up. The moment was gone.

'Your mum is back,' Enilo said, a slight tremor in her whispery voice.

'Oh!' Kuki felt disappointment creep into her belly. It spread and began to constrict her lungs, feeling like panic. 'Please don't go, Enilo. Can't you stay for dinner? My mum is really nice and I know she'll be so glad to meet you!'

Enilo shook her head. 'No, she will not! Believe me, the moment you tell your mum about me, our friendship will be over!'

Kuki shook her head in exasperation.

'Have you looked at me well?' Enilo picked up the hem of her short dress and pointed at her bare, dusty feet.

'My mum is not like that! I promise!' Kuki said.

But Enilo shook her head vehemently. 'No!' she hissed with such force that her thin voice was suddenly a growl. For a brief moment her eyes were dark, menacing dots.

Kuki caught her breath. But she must have imagined it. All she could see now in Enilo's eyes was worry. She sighed.

'OK. I won't tell my mum anything.'

Enilo gripped the window bars, looking strangely undecided. As if she too could feel the same rising panic at the thought of leaving.

'My mum hardly ever comes into my room,' Kuki said softly. 'If I go out to say hello, she'll go upstairs to her room to change and then into the kitchen. And Aunty, Dr D's sister, will come any moment too and they'll be busy cooking dinner. So we could actually be here undisturbed for another hour or even more. We could watch a film on my tablet and I could bring you some dinner?'

Enilo looked wistful, as if she would have loved to stay.

'Do you need to be back home at a particular time?'

Enilo looked at Kuki sharply, and Kuki felt the blood rush to her cheeks. She still wasn't sure if Enilo was homeless. But she also couldn't just assume it. She had to ask her.

'Yes, I have to be . . . somewhere . . . at night-fall.' Her voice was a tiny whisper and to Kuki's surprise she looked terribly afraid.

Kuki swallowed and took a quick breath. 'Enilo, where do you live?'

Suddenly there were footsteps in the corridor outside Kuki's room. Enilo's eyes widened. She glanced at the window but they both knew it was too late.

Enilo darted to the floor and disappeared beneath Kuki's bed just as the door opened.

'Hey, Kuki!'

'Hello, Mum! You didn't even knock!'

Her mum frowned. 'Well, I never knock!'

'Yes, that's what I mean! I could have been changing!'

'Oh, I didn't know I wasn't allowed to see you changing any more! So why didn't you lock the door?'

'Mum, you know what I mean!'

Her mum raised her hands in surrender. 'OK, OK, I'll try to remember to knock next time. You are right.'

'Can I come and help you do anything?' Kuki asked, hoping to get her out of the room.

But to her shock, her mum walked to her bed and sat down on it. Kuki's heart beat wildly. How she wished Enilo hadn't been so stubborn and had let her just introduce her to her mum. Now she felt like a criminal, hiding someone under her bed.

'How was your day, omo mi?'

'Oh, everything was fine, Mum.'

Her mum patted the bed beside her. Kuki had to be careful not to roll her eyes. How could her mum want to have a talk right now?

'I've been worried about you these past few weeks, Kuki.'

Kuki sighed.

'And don't you start rolling your eyes on me now. I am not being overly sensitive. It isn't normal for a thirteen-year-old to spend every afternoon alone in her room. You need friends and company and things to do!'

'Mum, I am fine, really!' Kuki tried to get up. Anything to end this conversation right now.

Her mum pulled her back gently but firmly. 'You said you didn't even have a single friend to invite to your birthday.'

Kuki shrugged, wishing the floor would swallow her up. Or Enilo, so she wouldn't have to listen to this awfully embarrassing conversation.

'Dr D and I were thinking maybe we could register you in a kids' club or some other afternoon activity. He could find out if there is anything like that around here. What do you think? You could meet other kids there and—'

'You spoke to Dr D about me?' Kuki looked at her mum in shock.

'Of course I did! He is part of our family now

and he is just as worried about you having issues fitting in at school.'

'I don't have issues fitting in at school!' Kuki snapped. She glanced at her rucksack in the corner but quickly looked away. Moji's bright-red notebook was sticking out of her bag like a red flag, telling her to stop lying.

'Kuki, please calm down. Dr D and I are just worried about you, that's all! He even had a serious talk with Aunty because of the way she has been harassing you. She didn't take it well. That's why she is not coming over this weekend.' Kuki's mum sighed.

Kuki stared at her. That definitely surprised her! Dr D had quarrelled with Aunty because of her? Well, maybe he'd done that because her mum had told him she was worried. Kuki couldn't really imagine Dr D worrying about her.

'You have changed since we moved here, you know,' her mum went on.

Kuki looked up sharply. Was that true?

'You are so reserved, often lost in thought. You hardly ever say anything at dinner. You used to be so much livelier! It's like you haven't really settled in.'

Kuki felt hot and uncomfortable under her mum's sad eyes. But she was also beginning to feel angry. It wasn't like anyone had actually asked her if she had wanted to move here. And yes, she understood that her mum wanted to be happy and all that, but she couldn't expect her to just switch into her new life in two seconds as if nothing had changed. As if her life wasn't upside down from one day to the next. She couldn't help it that she didn't make new friends easily, that Moji and Faith were horrible and that she and Dr D were awkward around each other. And, besides, wasn't it normal to need time to adjust? But before she could say anything, her mum stood up, supporting her belly with her hand.

'Just think about it, Kuki, OK? Being on your own every afternoon for hours till we come home isn't good for you.'

Kuki bit her lip and shrugged.

'Now come help me get the shopping into the house. And I will need help cooking dinner now that Aunty isn't coming.'

When Kuki returned to her room after emptying the car of her mum's shopping bags, she darted to her bed and flipped up the blanket.

Her belly flopped in disappointment.

Enilo was gone.

Dinner was quieter than usual. Aunty's empty chair seemed to fill the room, making her absence even more oppressive than her usual hawk-like presence. Kuki played around with her jollof rice, eating four grains at a time. She wasn't really hungry. Once in a while she stole a quick glance at her mum, who seemed lost in thought.

'Everything OK, Kuki?' Dr D asked.

She nodded and then tried to balance one more grain of rice on her fork. But the fifth grain kept on falling off.

'So, Kuki, what subject would you say is your best in school?' Dr D said suddenly after another round of silence.

Oh! This was more than the usual 'how was your day?'

'Ehm, I think English,' she said, feeling shy.

'How come?'

'Well, the teacher is funny.'

'Oh, really?' Dr D smiled and looked interested,

waiting for her to say more.

'He's just this very overexcited kind of person and he makes even the most boring old literature sound like a thriller.'

'Ha!' Dr D grinned. 'I had a teacher like that. That was Mrs Agbi for me. My biology teacher. She's the reason why I became a doctor. She made body organs and enzymes sound like the most amazing phenomena of nature – which they are, by the way! Don't let me start about the heart, how powerful it is and the incredible things it does in our body!' He grinned and looked like a ten-year-old as he did so. 'I felt like I had no choice but to study this wonder of nature in more detail.'

'You never told me that, D!' Mum said, waking up. 'I don't remember any of my teachers leaving such a big impression on me.'

'Well Mrs Agbi was amazing! She used to say: "More than sixty thousand miles long! Twice around the world! That's how long all our blood vessels are together. And your heart has the job of pumping blood through that entire jumble of veins all day long!"'

'Are our veins really that long?' Kuki asked.

'Yes! When they are all put together,' Dr D said. 'She always made us start every lesson with a good laugh. She'd say: "Everyone, do your hearts a favour and laugh please. As loud as you can!" And we'd all laugh as loud as possible. "Never forget your heart medicine!" she'd say. "A round of laughter sends twenty per cent more blood flowing through those veins!"'

Mum giggled. 'That's a good one, D,' she said, looking more cheerful.

Kuki smiled.

Dr D dropped his knife and fork on to his plate and clapped his hands together. 'I was actually planning to tell you the surprise after dinner, but since you ladies are looking in a better mood, I'll just do it right now.'

'A surprise?' Kuki asked, feeling confused because he was looking at her.

'Yes, I have a surprise for you, Kuki. A kind of late birthday surprise, sorry about the delay.'

'Oh.'

He jumped up and went to his doctor's bag which was in its usual corner near the front door.

He searched around in it and then came back holding some thin colourful strips of cardboard.

He laid them on the table beside Kuki's plate. Mum also seemed unaware of Dr D's plans because the surprise was written all over her face as well.

'Choose a colour,' he said.

'What?'

'For your room! We can't have you staying in that dreary old study of mine the way it is. We'll start by painting the walls.'

'Oh, that's a wonderful idea, D! With all the moving stress and preparations for the baby I hadn't even had time to think of that,' Mum said.

Kuki stared at them both, feeling rather overwhelmed.

'And as soon as the painters are through, we'll get rid of that hideous old leather chair and the desk, and get you some new furniture.'

'Thank you, Dr D,' she said.

'No sweat! Even if we have been quite busy, it's really about time that we have you feeling more comfortable in your new home.'

Kuki picked up the light-blue strip. It was the

bright blue of the ocean on a very sunny day. She stretched her hand, closed one eye and looked at the strip under the lamp. A bright-blue mosaic courtyard formed out of the cardboard and she could see a thin wisp of a girl stepping out from behind a tree. A nice, warm feeling filled her belly and spread out to her chest.

His words 'feeling more comfortable in your new home' resounded in her mind. It was the first time since moving to Dr D's that she actually considered the idea of house number fourteen being her home.

17

WHITE TRAINERS
WITH PINK STRIPES

'It's my turn now, Kuki, move over!' Joe grumbled.

Kuki stepped back hurriedly to allow him to look down the microscope. The biology lab smelt of onions and everyone was teary with runny noses. Thinking of Dr D's excitement about his biology teacher the night before, Kuki had tried to discover the infinite wonder of multi-magnified slices of onion. She hadn't really succeeded in feeling excited yet. But Mrs Akerele had told them they would investigate human skin under the microscope next time. Maybe that would be more spectacular.

She stretched her back and caught a pair of eyes

staring at her from across the lab. It was Faith. She had been trying to catch her attention all day. Kuki's belly tightened at the memory of their last embarrassing encounter. And to think that she had actually thought Faith had wanted to be her friend!

'So finish up, everyone,' Mrs Akerele called. 'Next week I will collect your essays on plasmolysis. And everyone clean up their utensils and tabletops. All the pipettes in here, please!'

Someone passed Kuki and dropped a piece of paper on the table she had just wiped clean. She looked up to see Faith hurry out of the lab.

'*I am sorry*,' the scribbled words said.

Kuki squeezed the paper in her fist. She didn't need the likes of Faith who only tried to be nice or said sorry in secret.

She snatched up her bag and then noticed Moji staring at her with a strange look on her face. Had she seen what happened? That was all she needed – Faith's stupid note getting her into trouble with Moji. She had to get rid of it immediately. She rushed out of the lab, almost hitting Mrs Akerele who was gathering pipettes.

'Careful now!' Mrs Akerele called crossly.

Kuki ran down the corridor, which was almost empty. Mrs Akerele's biology class always lasted longer than it should, which was annoying because it was the last class of the day. There was a bin at the main entrance – she could quickly slip the note into it. She squeezed through the groups of students chatting outside, put the note in the bin, and let out a sigh of relief, feeling safe. Glancing around, she jumped in shock.

Two dark-brown mean eyes were staring right at her. Kuki's heart slipped down into the dark-blue depths of her school uniform.

Moji.

'Why are you in such a hurry today?' Moji was not smiling.

'Oh, just erm . . . meeting a friend who is coming over to visit this afternoon.' Kuki felt quite proud of her quick response. She hadn't even needed to lie, since Enilo hopefully was going to come over later on.

They had reached the school gate now and all Kuki wanted to do was escape and run home. But she didn't feel brave enough to do so. So she let herself be interrogated by Moji.

'A friend!' Moji repeated in a nasty voice. 'What's her name?'

Kuki realized she had made a mistake. Moji probably thought she was meeting up with Faith.

'Oh, you don't know her. She's a . . . erm, family friend. My mum's friend's daughter.'

'Oh, really! Maybe I should come by this afternoon and join you and your friend! You could introduce me!'

Kuki's eyes widened in shock. The thought of Moji meeting Enilo was awful. She felt protective of Enilo and didn't want Moji making fun of her.

Kuki didn't reply. She just stared down at Moji's feet. She was wearing the same sandals that she had wanted to exchange with Kuki the other day.

'What are you staring at?' Moji hissed. She crossed her legs awkwardly, hiding one foot behind the other. Now Kuki saw something that she had not noticed before. Moji's sandals were frayed at the front and her toes were almost touching the floor.

She glanced up and saw embarrassment in

Moji's eyes. And pure hateful anger.

Moji was ashamed!

'You know what, since you were so eager to become friends with everyone last week, I think I know what you can do to prove you are worthy!' Moji spat out the words from between clenched teeth.

Kuki took a step back. 'I wasn't trying to—'

Moji pointed at Kuki's feet. 'Get me a pair in size thirty-nine, OK?'

'Wh . . . what?'

'It's my birthday next Tuesday. Perfect timing, don't you think? Get me my birthday trainers and you can join the club!'

'But I don't even want to join . . .'

Moji shot her a deadly look. 'With. Pink. Stripes. You better not disappoint.'

18

DRESSES, MAKE-UP

'What's your thing with shells?' Kuki asked as she helped Enilo into one of her mum's old dresses. The dress was so big, the shoulders so wide and the sleeves so flared, that Enilo all but disappeared into it.

Enilo shrugged. Today she had woven little cowries into her cornrows, and she was wearing bracelets of shells around her slender wrist.

'They are beautiful. And special.' She sounded wistful. 'I like to surround myself with them.'

Kuki waited. She had a feeling Enilo wanted to say more and hoped she would.

Enilo took the matching belt of the dress from Kuki and tied it around her waist. 'Shells are houses, you know. They are abandoned homes,' she said. 'Clams and mussels and many other sea creatures can actually create their own shell-homes. They are never homeless. Is that not amazing?' Enilo's eyes brightened briefly.

Kuki could hardly breathe. Was she going to talk about herself finally?

'All except the hermit crab,' Enilo continued, and now her eyes were glinting like hard black stones. 'They are fragile sea creatures that need protection from predators yet they cannot make their own home, even though they need one.'

'Oh,' Kuki said. 'How do they survive?'

'They have to find shells abandoned by others. They slip into them, make them their home until they outgrow them. Then they have to find a new one. They move from one home to the next, always on the lookout for a perfect one. Never ever feeling truly at home.'

Kuki glanced at Enilo, sensing a change of mood.

'I sometimes wonder what they think about that? They must be really angry at their luck.' Enilo bit her lip, then she picked up the flowery dress at the hem and walked to the tall mirror in the hall. 'How come you have all these big dresses?' she asked, twisting her waist and swirling the silky dress this way and that.

'They are my mum's from the nineties, I think,' Kuki replied as she put on hers with a sigh. Enilo had switched subjects again. 'I found a box with old clothes when we were moving here to Dr D's.'

'Why do you call him that?'

'His name is Dapo. D is for Dapo.'

'That's not what I meant,' Enilo said.

Kuki twirled around in front of the mirror too. She watched her dress flare open. It was much too long for her. When she noticed that Enilo was waiting for an answer she shrugged. 'I can't imagine calling him *Dad*. He isn't my dad. My mum met him at the hospital where she works. Everyone calls him Dr D, so I just joined in.'

'And he doesn't mind?'

'He never said anything. I think it would be awkward for him as well if I called him Dad.'

Enilo nodded, looking thoughtful.

'My dad . . . my real dad left us,' Kuki added quietly.

'That's sad.'

Kuki shrugged again. 'He wasn't a very brave person,' she replied. 'At least that's what my mum said.'

She swallowed, remembering the look in her mum's eyes the one night she had told Kuki the story of how her dad left. Mum had tried to sound unbothered, but Kuki had heard the hurt in her voice and seen the leftover strands of pain in her eyes. Kuki had been horrified to hear that her dad had left her mum when she was most vulnerable. Just after giving birth to her! Kuki had hugged her mum tightly and thought such wicked thoughts about her dad that she had been ashamed.

It was her dad who had given her the name Kokumo. He was to blame for the never-ending reminder of the past. And then, after giving her the name, just a few weeks later he had left.

'We were very young. He was a weak man and I think he just wasn't ready for a family yet,' her mum had said. 'When they told us that the chances of you surviving were very little, he just gave up. He had recently gotten an offer to study in Europe and so he left.'

He hadn't believed in Kuki or in the name

he had given her.

Kuki had told her mum that she hated her name because it sometimes made her feel anxious that something was wrong with her. But her mum had told her: 'Your name is not a sign of your weakness but the proof of your strength. You should be proud of it!'

'I am sorry about that,' Enilo said softly.

'I never got to know him, so I don't miss him,' Kuki said, walking to the window. 'And Dr D makes my mum happy. That's all that matters.' But every now and then, she did wonder where her father was, what he was doing, and if once in a while he thought of her. If he wondered about her like she did about him.

Enilo came to the window too and Kuki was surprised at the pain she saw in her friend's eyes.

'What about your parents?' Kuki asked gently. 'Where are they?'

Enilo immediately pushed away from the window. 'Why don't you show me this animal walk you talked about?' she said.

Kuki frowned. 'Animal walk? Oh, you mean *catwalk*!' She giggled. Sometimes Enilo was really funny. 'OK, watch me.'

Kuki pushed out her chest to the front and her bum backwards, tilted her chin upwards and walked across the room like she had seen models do. Her mum's dress swept the ground behind her like a bridal train.

Enilo snorted and raised an eyebrow. 'Was that supposed to be very special?'

Kuki giggled. 'Well, you try, and let's see if you can do it any better.'

Enilo went to one end of the hall and with a look so serious that it made Kuki choke with laughter, she began to hobble and stalk across the room. She looked like she had hurt her foot.

'Wait, I know what we need!' Kuki cried, giggling. 'High heels and make-up. Let's go raid my mum's bedroom!'

A line of worry furrowed Enilo's forehead.

'Hey, it's all right. She won't be home for two hours and she knows I often borrow her things. All she wants is for me to return anything I borrow.'

Enilo still didn't look convinced.

'It's really OK, just follow me.'

The light in the bedroom was subdued by the drawn curtains across the two windows.

Kuki went to her mum's dressing table and opened her beauty case. Her mum had this wonderful set of make-up that she rarely used. She only used her kajal every day. The beauty case came out on special occasions, when they went to weddings or when she and Dr D went out for some romantic dinner without Kuki.

'Hah, there it is,' Kuki said, grabbing it and jumping on the bed. 'Come and see, this set is amazing, there are four little drawers inside . . .' She looked up to see Enilo standing in the doorway and looking awkward. 'Look,' Kuki said, and Enilo edged into the room slowly.

'Wow!' she said, her eyes glinting as she saw the palettes that Kuki had spread out on the bed. 'But what do you use forty-eight different colours for if you have only two eyes? This case could belong to a box jellyfish. They have twenty-four eyes.'

'Ha-ha! It would need water-resistant make-up though!' Kuki laughed. 'They are not all eye-shadows. Some are blush for the cheeks.' She grabbed one of the brushes in the bottom drawer of the case and patted the bed beside her. 'Let me make you up.'

She brushed the mascara over Enilo's lashes. 'Wow, I think you have the longest lashes I have ever seen!'

Enilo did not reply. Her large eyes, which Kuki had framed with kajal, looked the deep purple of the ocean in the dim light of the room.

Enilo blinked and suddenly jerked. 'I . . . have to get out of . . . here!' she gasped. She clawed at her belly, whipping back and forth.

'Enilo! What's wrong?'

Enilo shook her head and fell on to the ground, curled up like a kitten.

'What is it?' Kuki asked, panic creeping up her throat.

Enilo shuddered and writhed. A tear trickled down her cheek.

Kuki thought frantically. Maybe she needed fresh air! She helped Enilo up and walked her out. Enilo's breathing steadied as soon as they left the room. She opened her eyes and rested her back against the wall in the hall. Kuki laid a hand on her arm. She noticed that her own fingers were trembling.

'Are you OK?' she asked gently.

Enilo looked almost lost. She nodded but glanced back nervously to Dr D and Mum's bedroom. She shuddered and hurried down the stairs.

'Do you want us to get out of here? Should we go to . . . your . . . ehm, the abandoned house?'

But Enilo whirled around abruptly. 'No!' she cried, much too loud. Her eyes were serious and panicked. 'I don't want to go there!'

Kuki stared at her in surprise.

'I . . . I can't go back there . . . it's too . . .' She swallowed and shook her head. 'Can I stay here?' Enilo's voice was now whispery and uncertain, like a baby bird chirping for the first time.

'Of course you can!' Kuki replied.

'I mean, for the night.'

'I'll ask my mum,' Kuki said slowly. 'I'm sure if she—'

'No,' Enilo said. 'Your mum cannot know!'

Kuki's eyebrows shot up. 'You mean that you sleep over in secret . . . and I don't tell anyone?'

Enilo looked at her, her eyes black and hard once more. She was disappointed; Kuki could feel it and her belly twisted nervously. She wanted to make Enilo happy.

'My mum is really nice, I wish you would believe me. We could call your mum and ask her . . .'

But Enilo was already shaking her head vigorously. 'No, no . . . your mum cannot know. She can never know!'

'But why?' Kuki asked.

'Trust me, like I already told you, the moment you tell your mum about me, our friendship will be over! I know about these things.' Kuki's mum's nineties dress had slipped from Enilo's shoulder and now it fell to the ground, showing her too-short dress beneath.

Kuki's eyes slipped down to Enilo's bare feet. She swallowed, feeling ashamed of her thoughts, but she understood what Enilo was saying. Would her mum be indifferent to these things? Kuki wasn't sure. She didn't believe that her mum would generally be against her having Enilo as a friend. But having her sleep over? Without having met or talked to her parents? Without knowing anything about her family? That was what she was worried about. Kuki sighed. She didn't want to deceive her mum, but she also didn't want to risk anything that would come between her and her newly found friend.

Enilo slowly stepped out of the dress heap on the floor. She handed it to Kuki. 'I understand,' she said. Her eyes were heavy with disappointment and her voice cold. 'I am sorry I asked.'

'No, wait,' Kuki said. 'It's OK! Let's do it!'

19

A GRITTY
LUNCH BREAK

K uki came down the stairs at break time wondering where to hide today. She wanted to go to her usual quiet spot at the shady tree near the side fence, but she could already see that there were a group of girls over there today playing ten-ten. They were laughing so hard because the girl whose turn it was was taking things too seriously. She was charging like a bull, almost in a frenzy, her braids jumping with her as she kicked out her feet.

Kuki sighed, wishing she could just join them. They looked younger than her but she wouldn't even have cared! As long as she didn't need to spend her break time hanging around with Moji and her friends, or being sent to get her something from the kiosk.

This morning, she'd had to carry Moji's bag again. She'd left the house too late because she'd been so preoccupied with thoughts of the night before.

Enilo sleeping over had been such fun. She had gone back to her room after dinner, with some snacks that she had smuggled out of the kitchen for Enilo. Then they had snuggled in her bed and spent half the night giggling quietly into the covers, talking, playing 'If I were a . . .', discussing their best films, books, music, animals. It had been so wonderful. Finally she really had a friend. A best friend. And she didn't care that Enilo wasn't the kind of best friend people usually had. And that she had a few too many secrets. Kuki was just happy.

But when she'd woken up in the morning, she'd been alone in bed. It had been a cold, disappointing, almost haunting feeling to wake up without Enilo. She had felt empty and weak without her, as if a vital part of her was gone.

Suddenly long waving arms caught Kuki's eye

from near the gate and she saw it was Moji gesturing for her to come over.

Oh no!

Kuki's chest tightened and her sudden, stupid reflex of wanting to turn around and escape sent her lunch box flying down the steps.

Of course it opened, and a meat pie and a bunch of boiled groundnuts scattered all over the place. Why hadn't she checked her box this morning? Her mum always included the weirdest things in it. Who cracked boiled groundnuts in their lunch break at school? Kuki wished she hadn't come out of class at all.

'Why does this only ever happen on days when one has groundnuts, right?' someone beside her said, and began helping her pick them up, one by one.

It was Sahid, one of the quieter kids from the back of class who never really said much. He grinned as he dropped a handful of nuts back into her box. It was a friendly smile but Kuki was too embarrassed and worried to respond. She shook off some grass, dirt and yucky pink chewing gum that were now stuck to the meat pie and dropped it back in the box, disgusted. She sighed. No lunch for her today.

Sahid stood waiting as if he wanted to chat. Chioma joined him. 'Should we go look for Joe and the others?' she asked. 'They're probably at the football field as usual.'

Sahid nodded. 'Do you want to come?' He was looking at Kuki.

Kuki was so surprised that she forgot to say yes. She just stared at him.

'Sahid, Chioma!'

A loud, bossy voice interrupted them and an arm fell heavily on Sahid's shoulder. Moji's arm. It tightened around Sahid's neck. He immediately wriggled out of the stranglehold and pushed Moji away, looking annoyed.

Kuki wished she could push Moji away. Why couldn't she just do the same?

'You guys have to see this!' Moji chirped in her super-sweet voice. 'Jenny has the Shuri graphic novel! And it's amazing!'

Sahid's face lit up at that.

'She's near the gate,' Moji said, and Sahid and Chioma hurried away to see the comic.

Kuki tried to move past Moji to follow them but Moji's hand shot out and pulled her back. 'What were you telling them?' Moji hissed. 'I hope you weren't talking about me!'

Kuki shook her head and frowned. What was Moji's problem? She really didn't understand why she was always on her case. Why couldn't she just leave her alone? But the words she so wanted to say wouldn't come out.

'I thought you were on my team?' Moji asked, her eyes glinting angrily. She moved closer and Kuki edged backwards, moving a step up.

What was Moji trying to say? Wasn't she allowed to talk to anyone else? Was she going to burst into every conversation Kuki had and ruin it for her?

Wistfully she remembered her first day of school here. How hopeful she had still felt then. Now things had not only gone to bad but to much worse. She felt almost faint.

Moji snatched the meat pie from her still-open lunch box. 'Oh, thank you!' she said, as if Kuki had offered it to her. She bit into it and walked off.

Kuki felt her muscles loosen with relief and then she smiled at the thought of Moji's gritty, nasty lunch.

20

CHOICES AND
DECISIONS

'Why do you do that?'

Kuki stopped writing and looked up. She was sitting at her desk copying her homework into Moji's exercise book.

'What do you mean?' she asked Enilo, who was lying on the floor and trying to fix some really tiny shells on to a thin band while reading a book at the same time.

'Why do you always do your homework twice?'

Kuki stiffened and thought frantically. She hadn't mentioned Moji to Enilo yet. She had often thought about it, especially in the past few days. Enilo had slept over every night since, and they had become so close. She realized now that she was ashamed. Enilo was such a strong person. She seemed so independent, not even needing her parents and just doing what she felt like. Kuki was sure she would be shocked to hear how she let Moji bully her in school.

'Ehm . . . I'm just helping out a . . . ehm . . . friend,' she said weakly.

Enilo sat up and dropped *Spirit Hunters* into her lap. She had decided to read all the scary books on Kuki's bookshelf, the ones that Kuki had bought but then felt too scared to read.

Enilo's eyes narrowed as if they were looking right through her lie. 'I have seen you do your homework twice so many times now, and I have seen you always write it into the exercise book of that Moji person. Why do you do their homework for them?'

Kuki shrugged, then drew a long breath. 'Moji is a girl in my class,' she said slowly. 'She kind of makes me do stuff for her. Stuff I don't want to do, like homework.' Kuki felt relieved to have finally told someone.

'But why do you agree to it?'

Kuki felt her cheeks flush. If only she knew the answer to that question! She had no idea why she was acting the way she was. Why she couldn't say no to Moji, why she was shy, found it difficult to make friends. She sighed. 'It's not that easy. She's quite . . . mean.'

'You shouldn't let her!'

'What do you expect me to do? If I don't do what she says, she'll only get more mean! Or turn everyone against me. And how am I supposed to stop her? She is this huge, tall, horrible person.'

'I cannot tell you how and I cannot make your decisions for you, but I definitely wouldn't let anyone else rule my life like that!' Enilo said. Her eyes glinted and for the first time Kuki saw contempt in them. 'There is a point when every person has to decide to stand up and fight for themselves. But this is obviously a decision that every person has to make for themselves.'

'Well, it's not that easy for everyone!' Kuki retorted. 'Not everyone is so bold and carefree or able to live their life how they want!' She stared at Enilo. 'Why do *you* hide here every night for days? Don't you have a family that is worried?

118

Someone who is looking for you? You're not doing anything about your fear or whatever it is that keeps you here!'

Kuki was shocked at her outburst and immediately wished she could take the words back. She was stunned at the sudden rage that had taken hold of her.

Enilo seemed to have turned to a pillar of rock. She didn't move an inch or even blink. She just sat there, her eyes hardening.

'I am sorry,' Kuki said eventually, turning back to her homework. She felt mean and ugly.

The room was so silent. It was as if she had shocked Enilo out of words and even out of breath. She tried to continue writing but hated herself more with every word that she wrote into Moji's book. She pushed away the even worse thought of how she was going to find the money for Moji's trainers.

'I have a family,' Enilo said suddenly.

Kuki had almost forgotten that she was in the room with her, so lost in her own thoughts and worries was she.

She hardly dared turn around, in her fear that

Enilo might immediately stop talking.

'But I only call them family because we are of the same home. Not because I feel in any way connected to them. They are wicked and every single day of my life, I wish I could swap families. I wish I could have been born into another life.'

'I am so sorry to hear that,' Kuki whispered, turning.

But Enilo shook her head sadly and stood up. 'I am the one that is sorry. You are right! I had no right to ask you that question, when I am being a coward. I am the one running away instead of facing the decision that I have to make.'

'What decision? Are you leaving now?' Kuki asked, immediately feeling the panic boil up in her chest.

'Yes, I am tired of hiding. I have to take care of something right now.' Enilo placed the bracelet she had made on the desk in front of Kuki. 'I have to make a choice between good and bad. Normally, the decision should be easy. But this time it is not. Because in this case good and bad are not so different from each other.'

Enilo looked stiff with worry and fear.

'What if good and bad are so alike that they have almost become the same, Kuki? What does one choose?'

Kuki picked up the bracelet and traced the delicate shells with trembling fingers. Where did Enilo manage to find such special, rare-looking shells? She had never seen cowrie shells in such beautiful shades of orange. Tears pricked the insides of her eyes. Why did she suddenly have the horrible feeling that this bracelet could be a goodbye gift?

21

FAMILY SATURDAY

'Deeee! Deeee!'

Dr D and Kuki jumped at her mum's angry voice, calling from outside. It was Saturday morning and they had been measuring Kuki's room for her new furniture.

Kuki frowned. How come she was back already? Wasn't she meant to be at the hair salon?

Dr D and Kuki hurried out of her room. The front door slammed as they entered the living room and Mum wobbled towards them as fast as her big belly would allow. She was holding something strange which dangled from her fingertips, her face drawn into a tight, disgusted frown.

The thing landed on the side table with a loud

thump and Kuki's mum placed her hands on her waist, wheezing angrily.

'What in heaven's name is that?' Dr D asked, scratching his head. 'And aren't you supposed to be having your hair done, darling?'

'Yes, I also thought I would be at the salon by now, but I almost had an accident because this –' she pointed at the thing – 'this . . . hideous thing, which was obviously hidden underneath my car seat, rolled out in the middle of traffic and gave me the biggest fright!'

'Oh my goodness, Grace,' Dr D cried. 'Are you OK?'

Kuki moved forward to get a closer look at the 'thing'. It looked like a coconut wrapped in strips of colourful cloth. Strange metal hooks had been woven into the cloth.

'But why do you seem so angry with me?' Dr D asked quietly. 'I am sorry I didn't check under your car seat, but as from now I will definitely—'

'That is not the point, D!' Mum rolled her eyes impatiently. 'The question is what that thing was doing under my car seat and how it got there!'

'I have absolutely no idea . . .' Dr D stammered.

'Well, I have a very good idea,' Mum said, marching into the kitchen.

Kuki and Dr D hurried after her and found her rummaging in the bin.

'Goodness, Grace, please calm down,' Dr D said, looking all flustered and worried. 'Why are you digging around in the bin?'

'There!' Mum cried and pulled out a black nylon bag that was covered in the oily remains of yesterday evening's rice and stew. 'I initially did not want to say anything because she is your sister and I feel bad enough that you always have to stand between us, so I just threw this away when I found it in our bedroom yesterday – underneath our bed!'

Her mum tore open the bag and a colourful bunch of chains, bracelets and other oddities tumbled out. Kuki now remembered where she had seen these. These were the chains that Aunty had wanted her mum and her to wear for protection! Mum had refused, so Aunty had smuggled them under Mum's bed!

Dr D suddenly went quiet. He turned to Kuki. 'Kuki, I want you to make your mum a cup of tea. Both of you, please wait here!' He turned to Kuki's mum. 'Bisola will pack her things immediately. I do not want to see her in this house ever again!'

Now Mum turned pale. 'D, there's no need to escalate up to that point! She is family and she is welcome here as long as she stops terrorizing us with her superstitious beliefs!'

'No,' Dr D said, his voice brittle with withheld anger. 'This has gone way too far!'

22

THE WRONG CHOICE

Kuki tiptoed through the dark corridor. The TV was on and the light of its screen flashed and dimmed through the gap in the living-room door. She peered through and saw Dr D and her mum snuggled together on the sofa. They looked very comfortable. Like they were definitely not planning to get up soon.

It had been a quiet and relaxed Sunday after the dramatic events of the day before. Even though Kuki had felt bad to hear Dr D quarrel with Aunty and then to see her storm out, she did have to admit to herself that the peaceful Sunday without her had been a relief.

Her heart began to thump now at the thought

of what she planned to do.

She had a choice to make. A choice between good and bad, just like Enilo. And she knew that whichever decision she took, it would have serious consequences. Whichever way, she was going to get into trouble. She sighed at the thought of Enilo. The two days without her had been . . . strange. She felt so miserable and so disconnected from everything around her, empty. And a strange panic overcame her every now and then. The fear that Enilo was gone.

She wondered what choice it was that Enilo had to make. Now Kuki wished she had told Enilo about her plans. Would Enilo have tried to talk her out of it?

Kuki realized that in the past weeks she had been making a lot of bad choices. Since she'd moved to Dr D's house she had become restless and uneasy. She had begun doing things she wouldn't have done before. She'd gone to the house of shells on her birthday, and come back after dark. She was being dishonest, cheating by doing Moji's homework. She was keeping secrets from her mum and Dr D and had even let Enilo sleep over without asking. And right now as she began to make her way upstairs through the dark stairway, Kuki knew that yet again she was definitely making the wrong choice. She felt it in every step she took. In the sluggishness of her feet and the heaviness of her heart. And yet she continued to make her way up the stairs. Her heart beat so loudly that she worried its beat would echo. She tried to move more quickly through the darkness to have it over and done with. But in her haste she missed a step and slipped painfully. She let out a tiny yelp of pain.

She listened in panic – was someone coming? – then steadied herself with an angry gulp. Why did her mum's purse have to be empty today of all days? She had had the perfect moment earlier while her mum had been in the kitchen and Dr D had been taking a shower. But her mum's purse had been a gaping, empty hole! She had almost thrown up into the purse in panic and had still felt so sick at dinner that she could hardly eat.

'Everything OK, honey?' her mum had asked, looking worried. And Dr D had spent dinner talking about how they would go about painting her room, and the new furniture shop that had opened up on Victoria Island that they could check for some 'teenager' stuff. He was being so nice and now she was going to pay him back for his niceness by stealing from him!

She had thought about asking for the money, but then she would have had to explain why. And she couldn't say she was buying someone a pair of trainers because she was being forced to!

She mustered up her last bit of courage and hurried into their room. She knew he had a torch on his bedside table for nights when there was a power failure. They all did. She groped around in the darkness until her fingers found it. Unfortunately she hit it with the back of her hand and the torch fell with a crash. She squeezed her eyes shut as it rolled underneath the bed, and listened for footsteps.

Everything was silent.

Goodness, she was the worst thief on the planet! She felt her eyes fill with tears of frustration and fear. But when they blurred her vision even more she realized how stupid she was being. This wasn't the moment for breaking down! She knelt down and felt around until she found the torch. She switched it on and began to search. Dr D's clothes were strewn across the bed but there was no wallet in his trousers. She found his leather work bag on the ground beside the bed and shone the torchlight inside.

Nothing!

Panic came over her. Did he leave it in the car? Or did he have it in his doctor's bag in the living room near the door? Would she have to stalk around the house later on when everyone was sleeping?

She shone the torchlight around the room, and when it landed on the dresser she saw it. A small but thick lump of leather! She slipped the torch between her chin and chest and fixed it there to free both hands. Then she opened the wallet. It was brimming with notes. Perfect! The more he had, the more unlikely he was to notice anything was missing.

She pulled out as many notes as she thought she would need.

Tomorrow, she swore to herself, she would put every single bit of change she received back into this wallet. And every month when she got her pocket money she would slip it into Dr D's wallet until she had paid everything back.

She was just about to place the wallet back on the dresser when she heard a noise. She whirled round, and in that very moment the lights went on.

23

DISAPPOINTMENT

At first Dr D just looked confused and surprised to see her. But then he looked from her face to her hands. He saw the money in one hand and the wallet in the other, and the look on his face changed to pure shock.

Kuki was rooted to the spot. Like a bush rat crossing the road and stunned by the headlights of a car, she stood there silently just holding the money and the wallet in furiously trembling hands.

Dr D took a step forward, cleared his throat and then shook his head. That was when Kuki saw the disappointment flooding his face. He had fully realized what was going on. She was a thief.

'I . . .' Kuki began but he immediately raised his hand to stop her.

Tears shot into her eyes like hot springs. She turned and dropped the wallet and money on the dresser.

Dr D went to her mum's wardrobe and took out a wrapper. 'I am going to go back downstairs and bring this to your mum,' he said, holding it up. 'She is waiting and I don't want her to come upstairs and see you here. Not now! Not when the baby can come any day soon, and not after yesterday! I do not want her worrying.' He drew a deep, disappointed breath before he continued, 'We will talk, Kuki. Some other time. When your mum is not around.'

And then he was gone.

Kuki leant against the dresser, too weak to move. She just stood there listening to Dr D's steps fade and disappear, just as his trust in her had disappeared. She had never felt more ashamed in her entire life.

She slunk back to her room weighed down with wretchedness. What would she do now? She had only made things worse. Now it was messed up at home as well as in school. She muffled a scream in her pillow.

If only Enilo were here! She walked to her window and shoved it open. The sky was beautifully lit with stars and an almost full moon, so she could clearly see the small stretch of garden in front. Everything was quiet and there was no one in sight. Enilo was making her own choice right now. And as Kuki stared at the dark sky with tears streaming down her face, she wondered if Enilo would have made a better decision than she had.

24

GHOSTWRITER

Kuki couldn't get that look on Dr D's face out of her head. Over and over again she saw it, that moment when he glanced from her face to her hands, when surprise at seeing her in the room changed to shock at seeing the money and wallet in her hand and then to disappointment. When he realized that she was a thief!

At school the next day she could hardly concentrate on the lessons and gave stupid answers when she was called up in class. Her mind strayed to Enilo every so often, wishing for her to be in her room, waiting for her when she got home. She didn't know how she managed but somehow she survived the day and it was last period. English with Mr Akinte was definitely bearable and the moment he strutted into the class, Kuki managed to cheer up a little.

The way he always beamed, his eyes bright and excited, one would think English was about chocolate ice cream covered with caramel sauce and sugary nuts, and not about ancient authors with outdated language who had long turned to dust in their graves. Even Mr Akinte's clothes were bright and excited. Today he was wearing the loudest red shirt she had ever seen on a human being. Kuki loved his class.

'So, my dear students and fellow explorers of the wide and exciting terrain of literature, I am happy to announce that we will be starting a new topic today.' He placed his hands on his hips and, visibly brimming with excitement, announced: 'Biographies!'

Groans came from everywhere around the class and Mr Akinte raised his arms and shook his head in feigned shock.

'Now, now, don't you be deceived and think of biographies as some boring topic. The most inspiring books that I ever read were biographies of some of the world's most intriguing people.

Biographies can be absolutely fascinating pieces of literature.'

More groans.

Mr Akinte lifted his arms again. 'Patience, patience, all ye doubtful scholars,' he grinned. 'This time our analyses will go beyond the lives of our beloved poets and famous writers.' His voice sounded conspiratorial, as if he were telling them the world's best-kept secret. 'The biographies of all kinds of world-changing and mind-blowing people have been written. Of course, not every famous person with a life worth talking about is also a good writer. So someone else, a ghostwriter, writes their biography for them in the most interesting way possible for others to read.

'Now what I want everybody to do, is to start thinking about interesting famous people. Next week I'll write down your suggestions and we'll vote to choose one biography which we'll analyse in the next weeks.' He looked around as if he was expecting applause.

Kuki saw Moji slide a piece of paper to Joe and giggle when he grinned.

'Moji! Will you stop disrupting my lesson!' Mr

Akinte called, his forehead creasing.

'Can we really choose anyone, like Lil Nas X or Wizkid, for example?' Joe asked.

'Lil what?' Mr Akinte asked and everyone laughed.

Mr Akinte grinned. 'As long as this Lil-something person has a biography *and* your suggestion wins the vote, then I don't care whose biography it is.'

'I'm voting for Wizkid,' someone called.

'I'm choosing Teni,' Moji called.

'OK now, everyone quiet please,' Mr Akinte interrupted. 'Everyone can think of who they want to vote for till next week but please check first if they have a biography.'

Mr Akinte clapped his hands together. 'Now, your homework for this week is: writing your *own* biography!'

Now the groans were really loud.

'Be creative, children. What are the important milestones of your lives so far? What makes you interesting as a person? Who are your family members? What are your major accomplishments or hobbies or dreams or fears? I'm sure nothing will stop your imagination from blooming here and I look forward to reading your biographies! By Wednesday please.'

Final bell rang and school was over. Kuki grabbed her things and hurried out of class. She had almost made it to the gate when she heard her name.

Nooo! she thought as she recognized the voice. *Not today!*

'Why are you rushing out so fast?' Moji called. 'You forgot to pick up my exercise book for English homework.'

'But we are meant to write our biography!'

Moji shrugged. 'So?'

'How am I supposed to know about *your* biography? That's . . . something personal that only *you* can write,' Kuki stammered.

'Says who? I am definitely not going to write out my private life for any teacher to read, so if I were to write it I would invent a story anyway.'

Kuki shook her head, wondering how she was going to get out of this one.

'And besides, like Mr Akinte said, ghostwriting is common practice among famous people when it comes to writing their biographies.' She tapped her chest smugly when she said 'famous people' and wriggled her eyebrows.

Kuki stared at her in shock.

'Just be a bit creative and think up something nice for me,' Moji went on. 'I see you always writing stories in your book during break, and you are the best in class in English. Just make me look cool, OK?' Moji held out the book to Kuki with a raised eyebrow.

Kuki felt like screaming. She felt so ashamed, allowing Moji to bully her like this. Also she felt strange, as if she was being watched.

At the fence beside the large cashew tree she saw a shadow. A thin, barefoot girl in a short dress . . .

What . . .

She blinked. Was she imagining things?

A second later the shadow at the tree was gone. She must have imagined it. Enilo would never have come to a crowded place anyway. Kuki felt more alone than ever as she stared at the empty spot at the tree.

She was forced back to the reality of her

situation by a notebook being forced into her hands.

Moji walked away and towards the gate. And just when Kuki let out the breath she had been holding tightly in her chest, Moji turned and called: 'And I'm really looking forward to my birthday gift tomorrow!'

25

THE WORST WAY TO SOLVE YOUR PROBLEMS

Kuki glanced at her alarm clock. It was almost six. She sighed and tossed around in bed. She had hardly slept and had woken up several times drenched in sweat and worry at the thought of going to school.

There was no way she was going to go to school without the gift for Moji! Not to mention the biography she had to ghostwrite for tomorrow.

She realized she had a dilemma. She had to make her next choice, and again she knew she was making the wrong decision. She couldn't run from Moji for ever. Eventually she would have to go back to school and face her.

But not today, she thought with growing worry and bellyache as she lay in her bed. Come to think of it, she actually did feel physically ill. She could just call in sick. But Kuki didn't want to have her mum worrying. Her alarm would ring any moment and soon after her mum would come and check if she was awake. Kuki had never called in sick! Other than the time when she had fainted at the age of six, she'd never missed school.

When her mum knocked and popped her head through the door Kuki had a solution.

'Mum, I hardly slept at all last night!' she said. And it wasn't even a lie. 'Do you think I could stay home today? I can hardly keep my eyes open.'

Her mum hurried towards the bed and sat down on it, placing her cool hand on Kuki's head. Kuki noticed it was trembling.

'Mum, I'm fine, really! I don't feel ill or anything. I just couldn't sleep. I shouldn't have drunk so much Coke late yesterday evening, that's all. I think that's what kept me up.'

Her mum looked unsure at first then slowly

nodded. 'OK, I'll call the school and tell them you won't be coming in today. And you make sure that doesn't happen again, Kuki. We can't have you missing school for such reasons.'

Kuki nodded quickly.

'Will you be OK, staying home alone all day?'

'Mum! I am thirteen!'

'OK, OK, sorry, I forgot!' her mum said.

'And besides, I have to write a biography so I'll just work on that when I get up later.' Kuki didn't add, 'And I have to write a second biography for my bullying classmate as well.' She felt her cheeks burn with shame at the thought. Her mum gave her a kiss on the forehead. She smelt so good and Mum-like that Kuki suddenly felt tears burning in the corners of her eyes. She held her mum tightly and wished she could tell her everything. Dr D had obviously not told her about the stealing, and Kuki definitely wasn't going to either!

Her mum hugged her back. 'Are you really OK, honey?'

Kuki nodded quickly, glad it was still dark in her room and that her mum couldn't see her tears.

As soon as her mum left the room Kuki let out

a sigh, relieved that she didn't need to face Moji today. Then she buried herself deep into her pillow and slept for the rest of the morning.

It was the eeriest dream. She was strolling along the beach, the waves washing lazily over her bare feet, when she suddenly heard voices in the distance. Children's voices and laughter. She saw heads bobbing in the water and arms waving.

'Come,' the voices called, and she knew it was her they were calling. She felt overcome by a strange urge to join them but she shook her head, not sure about the waves and feeling something was wrong about the kids.

But an enormous wave came after her and swept her off her feet. At first the water was warm and gentle on her skin, swirling around her like a cosy blanket, its soft fingers gently prodding her towards the children in the distance. She allowed the water to take her into its gentle embrace.

But after a while something changed. The water became thicker and heavier and seemed to be losing its blue colour. Swimming became difficult, like fighting through honey. The children were now really close. Kuki tried to swim away from them, but she could hardly move and soon she was surrounded by them. They were strangely beautiful and seemed to glow as the milky water dripped off their dark-brown faces like glistening pearls. They had thick, shiny black hair and large eyes that could have been beautiful but which glinted cold and mean. The children began to close in on her.

Kuki tried to struggle towards the shore. But even the sandy beach had now changed. Bright clumps made it look like a coral reef. It was too colourful, too bright . . .

She began to panic and the laughter behind her began to sound menacing. Then she heard a whispering voice, calling to her. Beyond the beach was the abandoned house of shells, with its silvery, twisted tree. And in the branches sat Enilo.

A hand grabbed her foot. Kuki screamed in horror as she was tugged underneath the waves.

She woke up gasping for air, coughing and spluttering, as if she had been drowning in real life.

26

HAUNTED

Kuki hurried down the path to the house of shells.

Enilo had been gone for three days.

Waking up after that awful dream had made her realize how much she had missed her and that she was worried about her. She had worked on her biography but her thoughts were taken up by Enilo. When she'd finished as best she could and it was time to write Moji's biography, she'd remembered Enilo's whispery voice asking, 'Why do you always do that?' She'd flung Moji's notebook into the corner of her room. And soon after she'd found herself walking down the path to the abandoned house.

Kuki worried about her friend. What if she was

gone? Of course she wanted to be happy for Enilo and imagined her being back with her family, wherever they were. But what would that mean for their friendship? Would Enilo even have come to say goodbye? Or what if she'd come to some harm? Kuki walked faster at the thought.

She ran the last stretch of forest. To her relief, everything was calm. Nothing appeared strange to her.

As soon as she arrived at the gates she saw Enilo. She was sitting between the two dancing statues in front of the house, staring right at Kuki from the moment her hand touched the rusty, moss-covered gates. Almost as if she had been expecting her.

Instinctively, Kuki knew Enilo wasn't happy that she had come. Her relief at finding Enilo immediately turned to worry.

Sweat gathered at her temples. Even though it was already late afternoon, the sun was still throwing down the heat in waves and she felt as if she were standing under a huge toaster. Kuki wiped her face and squeezed through the gate.

Her trainers crunched the shells strewn across

the driveway as she approached, breaking the heavy stillness.

Enilo made no move to get up or say anything. She just watched Kuki with wary eyes.

'You've been gone for three days,' Kuki said. She hadn't wanted it to sound like a reproach, more like an explanation for her sudden appearance. But it did.

Enilo shrugged.

'Did you take care of . . . the things you wanted to, ehm, take care of?'

'Not yet,' Enilo said with a frown. 'And you?'

Kuki shook her head. 'I got myself into trouble. Dr D wants to have a serious talk with me. And tomorrow in school I'll have to face Moji.'

'Hmmm,' Enilo said. She seemed lost in thought.

Kuki immediately felt terrible. Here she was, going on about her problems and feeling wretched about herself when Enilo probably had it much worse. She wished Enilo would tell her everything, or anything.

'The house must have been so beautiful once,' Kuki said, changing the subject.

'I love it the way it is now,' Enilo replied abruptly. She stood up, leaving the shade of the entrance, and stared up at the house. 'Things don't need to be new and shiny for you to love them.'

Kuki bit her lip, feeling like a snob even though that was not what she had meant.

'The house may be abandoned yet it refuses to give up! No one and nothing, not even time, can take away its heart.'

Kuki stared at Enilo in surprise. She wondered if Enilo was really talking about something else.

Enilo continued, 'The beauty and the good that is in something will always shine through . . . no matter what . . .' Her hands clenched into fists for a split second, then the moment passed. She glanced at the sky and turned to Kuki. 'Let's go to the beach!'

Kuki had hardly made sense of the sudden switch of mood and topic before Enilo disappeared into the dark gap of the half-open front door.

'Why would anyone abandon such a beautiful place, anyway?' Kuki asked as she ran in after her. She swerved as she noticed a family of lizards lined up on the wall. The big one with the bright-orange head nodded as if agreeing with her that this place was too lovely to be abandoned.

'Nobody wants to have it now,' Enilo whispered, as if not to hurt the house's feelings.

Kuki lowered her voice as well. 'Why?'

'Well, there are two stories and both of them make the house unattractive for anyone.'

'Oh, tell me,' Kuki said eagerly.

'Well, one story is that the house was built on the wetlands without a good foundation. It is too close to the ocean and every now and then an ocean surge sweeps in and floods the house.'

Kuki's nose was already filling with the damp smell of mould and she was sweating from the stickiness of the air inside the house. There was a puddle of water in one corner of the grand hall. The walls seemed to have more cracks today than when last she was here. Kuki could almost feel it groan in the heat.

'Yes, makes sense,' she said, following Enilo towards the mirrored room.

'That's the first story.' Enilo's voice was a whisper and yet it echoed strangely through the house, carrying across the hall up to the rooms like a wind swishing across beach sands and through treetops.

'The second story says that the house is haunted.'

Kuki stopped. She was standing right in the middle of the mirrored hall, staring at the wide-eyed reflections of her face all around her.

'Haunted?' she asked, gulping as her reflections asked the same question. She turned around, looking at herself in each mirror, and stiffened. Enilo was nowhere to be seen. In none of the mirrors!

She jerked her gaze out of the mirrors and realized she was alone. Her heart was suddenly beating wildly and she dashed for the door.

The corridor that led to the back was empty.

'Enilo!' she called, afraid to raise her voice to more than a whisper. 'Enilo!'

She took a deep breath. *No need to be foolish.* She'd been here before and never noticed anything strange. And anyway she wasn't superstitious. She did not believe in things like ghosts and haunted houses, just as she did not believe in

Abiku spirits possessing children. Those were all old myths.

She forced herself to walk to the back door in a slow and composed manner.

The sun was blinding after the dim light inside the house. Kuki squinted and held her hand up to shield her eyes.

Enilo was already crossing the tiny blue mosaic tiles of the terrace. She brushed the silvery trunk of the old, gnarled tree with the tips of her fingers as she passed.

'What did you mean by saying the house is haunted?' Kuki called.

Enilo turned abruptly and placed a finger to her lips. Her eyebrows were knitted to a sharp frown. She motioned Kuki to follow her.

Kuki crossed the blue mosaic, noticing that it had many gaps where the mosaic was missing or had chipped off. Some of them had been replaced with little bluish shells. They were really pretty and Kuki smiled. 'Where did you find these shells? They're so pretty,' she called.

But Enilo had already disappeared between the wild hibiscus and tall elephant grass ahead.

Kuki hurried after her, also passing beneath the tree. It gave a cool shade. Almost cold. A rustling above reminded her of the strange red fireflies that had dotted the tree the last time she had seen it. She hurried out of its shade, and fought through the grass and some thorny rose bushes as she tried to find the way through.

Soon she recognized a tight, overgrown path between the bushes and caught sight of Enilo ahead. She glimpsed blue ocean through the greens of the leaves. The path widened as the plants thinned out and the ground became sandier. The ocean now came into full view and the swishing of waves became a roar.

'Wait!' Kuki cried with an excited giggle.

But Enilo was already running across the soft glistening sand and into the water.

'This is wonderful,' Kuki cried. 'A private beach!'

There was not a single person in sight. Where the beach curved out of sight a boat was wedged into the sand beneath some coconut trees. Kuki flung off her trainers and ran swiftly across the hot sand to join her friend.

Enilo was waiting for Kuki, her eyes gleaming with mischief. She was knee-deep in the water and the waves crashing in had already wet her dress. Suddenly she bent down and dipped her hands into the ripples. Kuki wasn't quick enough and cold water slapped her in the face.

'Ah, you are so going to regret that!' Kuki cried and splashed water on Enilo. Soon they were screaming and soaked.

They fell, dripping wet, on to the beach. Even though the sun had begun to make its way down the sky, the sand was still too hot to lie on. Kuki squealed as they tried to dig into the cooler sand beneath but that didn't help.

But the spot beneath the coconut trees was heavenly. It was cool in the shade and the little boat, with its two benches, was the perfect chilling spot. A black plastic bag was tucked beneath one bench, and a net and a long machete had been thrown into the back of the boat.

Enilo immediately knelt in the sand and began sifting through it, picking out shells and checking them for blemishes.

Kuki joined her and they soon had a large

collection piled up in a heap.

'What kind of shells are these?' Kuki asked.

'These fan-shaped ones are scallops,' Enilo said. 'And these ones with the deeper ridges here are cockle shells.'

Kuki nodded and took a cockle shell from her to look at it more closely.

'Can you see these other lines that run right across the shells, in different-coloured stripes?'

Kuki nodded.

'Those are growth rings. So you can tell how old a clam or a scallop was before it died. This one here must have died very young, see: it has just a few rings.'

'Oh, that's sad,' Kuki said.

'Clams live much longer. Some actually live to be hundreds of years old.'

A sudden crack and a tumbling sound made them both jump. A greenish-brown coconut thumped into the sand. It looked fresh and its skin was shiny and unbroken. Enilo clapped her hands in delight and ran to pick it up. She shook it while holding it close to her ear to listen for the water inside.

'They rarely ever fall off on their own, unless they are rotten. But this one sounds good,' she said.

Then she walked to the boat and pulled out the machete. With swift skilful movements she sliced off the thick fibrous skin. Then she placed it on the deck of the boat and split it open. Fresh white flesh showed and sweet water trickled out. She handed Kuki a chunk of coconut with a triumphant grin.

Kuki climbed into the boat and made herself comfortable on the wooden bench. She could still see the house of shells. The arched windows of the top floor made the old mansion look like it was peering down at them, watching them over the bushes and trees.

'Why did you say it is haunted?' Kuki asked again.

'Because it is!' Enilo said with a shrug. She was sorting through more shells.

'How?'

'In the daytime it might be OK to be there but you should never *ever* go there at night!'

Kuki raised an eyebrow as she munched the

coconut. It was delicious.

'You don't believe me?'

Kuki grinned. 'I don't believe in ghost stories.'

'You should. This one is true. They call to me, after dark.'

Kuki stared at Enilo, not sure what to make of this. But then she remembered the evening she'd run away from the house of shells, the strange sounds like laughter in the forest. She swallowed, feeling her confidence crumble a little.

'That's the second reason why no one wants to buy the house. They say the owner died of grief. It was the Abiku that did it to him. They took all his children from him.'

Kuki sat up abruptly in the boat. 'I don't believe stories of Abiku either,' she said.

'The man and his wife moved away,' Enilo went on. 'But they say the man came back to sleep one last night in the house and in that night he died of grief. And now the house is haunted.'

'What a rubbish story!' Kuki cried. 'Abikus do not exist!'

Enilo shook her head grimly and then stepped into the boat beside Kuki. 'Don't say things you have no idea about!' Her eyes burnt with intensity. 'Let me tell you the story that I was once told.'

27

THE WORLD
OF THE ABIKU

'Someone . . .' Enilo began. 'A . . . a friend I knew very well . . . once told me about the Abiku. He knew these things because he was possessed by one.'

Kuki snorted, not believing and not sure if she even wanted to hear the story. But Enilo's gaze was so grave that Kuki sighed inwardly and listened as Enilo continued.

'There was once an enchanted world. A spirit world so beautiful that it was almost painful to behold. A place deeply connected with the spirit children, the Abiku, that lived in it. The world was beautiful but it was not kind. It lived off the hearts of the spirit children.'

Kuki raised an eyebrow. 'What do you mean?'

'Every time an Abiku goes to the human world to possess a child, a crumb of their heart is lost to the Abiku world. And it's these heart crumbs that make the spirit world so beautiful.'

'So why would the Abiku even leave their world if it is so wonderful?' Kuki pressed. 'Why don't they just stay there and keep their heart crumbs and leave us in peace?'

Enilo's face hardened. 'It is easy to judge others when you are in a good position! The Abiku world only seems beautiful. But it is a world that takes all the beauty and everything that makes life worth living for itself. The Abiku live without heart!'

She glanced at Kuki then stepped out of the boat again, as if sitting while talking was unbearable.

'This friend . . . said that the Abiku possess a child, become a part of it so they can enjoy the true beauty of the human world. They can feel, they can laugh, cry, learn and grow. All the things that are not possible in their world. But the connection to their spirit world is very strong. The spirit world draws them back too soon. And when that happens they hurt the human child they leave behind.'

'The child dies!' Kuki said.

Immediately a cold breeze swept over them, carrying her words away from her mouth and across the ocean, as if it couldn't bear for the terrible words to remain hanging over their heads.

'But how can they do that?' Kuki cried. 'How can they live with themselves?' She was beginning to tremble now. The sun had lost all its power and was sinking fast beyond the horizon. Her wet dress was almost dry but it still clung to her body like an annoying second skin.

'Their world steals bits of their hearts, crumb by crumb with every visit to the human world. The Abiku become cold and mean and one day they become totally heartless. Like empty shells. It doesn't matter to them that they hurt the children. They don't care any more. They come and go as they please.'

Enilo's eyes seemed glazed and wet, and Kuki realized with shock that she was fighting tears.

'Your friend . . .' she said quietly. 'What

happened to him?'

Enilo turned away, her shoulders trembling. 'Kuki, there is something very important I need to tell you . . . oh no!'

'What is it?' Kuki asked.

Enilo glanced over her shoulder. When she turned back to her, away from the setting sun, there was panic in her eyes. 'Quick!' she hissed, grabbing Kuki's arm and pulling her out of the boat.

Kuki managed to grab her trainers before Enilo broke into a run, pulling her along the beach and up the path towards the house. She ran as fast as she could, heart pounding, even though common sense told her they were being foolish.

'What is it?' she puffed. 'Why are we running like this?'

But Enilo didn't reply. At the bushy path she let go of Kuki's arm. She placed a finger to her lips and then ran through the bushes. Kuki quickly slipped into her trainers. The sky was grey and heavy with the coming night already. How quickly the afternoon had slipped away. She was sad that the day had ended and wished

Enilo would relax. Up ahead the drooping windows of the house looked like mournful eyes. No! This was just a gloomy old house. It wasn't haunted. Houses weren't haunted. Abikus did not exist.

Kuki stumbled after Enilo. But it wasn't as easy as before, now that it was dark. Thin branches and thorns scratched her arms relentlessly. She squealed as something dark and furry ran over her foot.

Enilo was waiting for her at the edge of the blue mosaic terrace. She was looking around nervously and beckoned Kuki to follow her quickly into the house. Kuki couldn't hear or see anything strange.

The only sounds were of the ocean in the distance and the rustling of the wind in the tree.

Kuki stepped into the house but turned back one last time. She suddenly had a strange feeling of being watched. But she could see no one in the shadows.

The early moon had come out and its light seemed to be dancing on the crown of the tree! Or was it the crown of the tree that was a dancing mass of leaves? Kuki shuddered.

But there was no time to see more. The fact that the moon was out meant it was past her curfew.

She had to run.

28

FRIEND OR FOE?

There was no car parked in front of the house! Kuki almost danced with relief. Only the fact that she was totally out of breath stopped her.

'Lagos traffic is good for some things,' she said wickedly, and saw Enilo's teeth flash briefly in the darkness.

They had run all the way back home. They had not stopped once or said a single word.

Enilo flitted quickly through the gate and Kuki followed, surprised she wanted to come in.

The light in the corridor was on. Kuki frowned. She must have left it on all day.

'We have to talk, Kuki!' Enilo said as soon as they were in her room. She picked up Moji's notebook from Kuki's desk. Kuki sighed and tried to take it from her. But Enilo held on to it. 'Kuki, you have to listen to me! We . . . we have to fight . . . for ourselves . . . for our lives!'

'What are you talking about?' Kuki stared at the book in Enilo's hand, feeling ashamed and knowing that Enilo was right. But she knew that this wasn't only about her doing Moji's homework for her. There was something else that Enilo was trying to tell her.

'We can't let others spoil our lives! If we know something is not right we should fight against it! We should be able to do that! Don't you think so? Shouldn't we feel it in our hearts?' Enilo held the notebook against her heart. Then she slammed Moji's book on to the desk.

Kuki had never seen Enilo so beside herself. She was always so strong-willed, reckless as if she didn't have a care in the world. All that talk about the Abiku and the house of shells being haunted must have really gotten to her. She must really believe it. But then why was she always hanging around there?

'Kokumo!'

They both went rigid at the call.

'Aunty!' Kuki gasped. What was she doing here? Hadn't Dr D told her not to come any more? Then Kuki remembered the corridor light. She must have arrived in the afternoon while she had been out!

Enilo just made it behind the door as it swung open to reveal Aunty, her head crowned with a high glittering gele.

'Why did you not answer me?'

'Sorry, Aunty, I was, ehm . . . listening to music, I had my earphones in. I didn't know you were back,' Kuki stuttered nervously.

'I only came to pick up some clothes that I had forgotten in the washing.' Aunty peered into the room and Kuki hoped she wasn't planning to come in. Enilo's slim figure was squeezed behind the door.

'How have you been, Kokumo?' Aunty looked almost worried.

'Fine, thank you,' Kuki replied.

'My brother has been angry with me. He said that I make you scared about evil spirits, and that you have other worries already.'

Kuki stared at the floor not knowing what to say.

'It is because I am worried about you that I say these things. I know my brother and your mother do not believe in Abiku. They say they are stupid superstitions, but I know what I am talking about! There are things in this world that affect us that we cannot see. Spirits and magic!' Aunty leant against the door frame and folded her arms across her chest. The bangles on her arms rattled.

Kuki sighed inside. Aunty didn't look like she was planning to leave anytime soon. Enilo was stiff against the wall and she looked sick with fear.

'When the goddess Oshun told me I could not bear children, I was shocked at first. But she did it for a reason,' Aunty said. 'I know that now. The Babalawo I consulted told me. Oshun did it so I would spend my life caring for other people's children and for children without parents. Oshun is the mother of orphans and lost children, did you know that?'

Kuki nodded quickly. Of course she knew the Yoruba gods and goddesses from old myths and legends. But she also knew that these were just old myths. And yet Aunty's eyes were serious –

she obviously believed every word that she was saying.

'So I have a plan!' Aunty paused, raised a finger and smiled so brightly that Kuki saw all her teeth at once, all the way to the big molars at the back. There was a red stain on her front tooth from her shiny lipstick. 'I have decided to marry!'

'Oh . . .' Kuki said cautiously. 'That's wonderful! Ehm, I didn't know you had a, ehm, boyfriend. I mean, ehm, fiancé . . .'

'Ahn-ahn, no, I don't have a fiancé yet,' Aunty retorted. 'I still have to select one!'

The way she said it made Kuki think of a basket of mangoes at the market and Aunty digging around in the basket, prodding the mangoes to select a good-looking one.

'But anyway my fiancé and I will adopt a child. That is the plan,' she said.

'Oh, that's nice,' Kuki said. She was really desperate now for Aunty to leave.

'So, what I am trying to say,' Aunty continued, 'is that it is my duty to protect any child I see that needs help. It is my duty to protect you and make sure nothing happens to you!'

Kuki nodded. 'I really am OK, thank you, Aunt—'

'Never doubt it,' Aunty interrupted. 'The Abiku exist. They are wicked things that make families miserable. The worst kind of spirit! Your mother, being pregnant, has to watch out! You and your mother, you both deserve to be happy and free of these heartless creatures!'

Kuki nodded again. 'I do feel very free of them, Aunty,' she said quickly. This was the second time within just a few hours that she was hearing this. First Enilo, now Aunty.

'Where are the earrings I gave you for your birthday? Why are you not wearing them?'

'Oh, ehm . . .' Kuki thought quickly. 'They are in the living room,' she said, remembering she had seen them recently on the bookshelf. She took a step towards the door. Maybe she could lure Aunty away from her room.

But Aunty just moved aside to allow her to pass.

Kuki ran to the living room and snatched the earrings from the bookshelf. Then she hurried back and sighed with relief that Aunty was still standing in the doorway.

'Here,' she said, and held out the earrings to Aunty.

'Well, go on, wear them,' Aunty said.

Kuki fumbled them into her earlobes with nervous fingers and rolled her eyes ten times in her mind until Aunty finally nodded.

'Lovely,' she said. 'Leave them on. They will protect you.' She raised a finger again. 'If you feel in any way strange, as if you are not yourself, tell me! Have you heard me? If there is an Abiku living inside of you we have to drive it out. Believe me. It is a wicked, heartless creature with not a crumb of good in it!'

Kuki nodded emphatically. 'I will.'

And then, to Kuki's immense relief, Aunty nodded and was finally gone.

Kuki closed the door and leant her head against it. 'Goodness, that was close,' she whispered.

She turned to look at Enilo when she heard no reply from her. Enilo looked very ill. Her eyes were wide and blurred with tears.

'What is wrong?' Kuki asked, shocked. But she already knew it. 'I am sorry,' she said. 'I should have warned you. Aunty thinks I am possessed by an Abiku. I know you believe they exist, but I don't.'

But Enilo shook her head and edged away from her as if she were a monster.

Kuki's stomach twisted. 'Can we just talk, please?' she asked. 'Why don't you ever talk to me? Who was it that told you the story of the Abiku? Did something happen to him? Nothing will happen to me! Really, you can trust me on this one, Enilo. I am not possessed by an Abiku. I would know!'

'Kokumo!' Aunty was calling again and Kuki groaned. She went to the door and pulled it open.

'Yes,' she called back.

'Who are you talking to?' Aunty said. She was walking briskly towards Kuki.

Kuki's heart missed a beat. She tried to close the door but Aunty pushed past her and burst into her room. Kuki closed her eyes, awaiting the outburst.

'Why are your eyes closed?' Aunty asked.

Kuki opened her eyes and looked around. Enilo was gone and the window was open.

She let out a burst of breath.

Aunty was watching her strangely. 'Every time I think you are all right, you do another strange thing to make me worried all over again.'

29

THE TALK

'**K**uki, your mum and I are trying our best to give you everything you need. Whenever you ask for anything, I mean, anything . . . we get it for you!'

Dr D sat on the sofa across from Kuki. His newspaper that he usually read back to back was thrown carelessly aside and he sat rigid opposite her. He wasn't enjoying this talk any more than she was.

Kuki wished she could dissolve into the air around her. She had never felt so ungrateful as in this moment.

'You get pocket money every month, for goodness' sake! Why didn't you just ask if it isn't enough? I can't believe you would actually steal—'

'I didn't mean to!' Kuki interrupted him. She couldn't bear hearing him say the word. 'I mean, I know that's what it looks like, but I promise, I swear, I really meant to give it back. I just wanted to borrow it!' Her voice quivered and she knew that tears were close.

Dr D did not look very convinced and shook his head. 'Why would you need so much money in the first place?'

Kuki sighed. She was going to have to tell him the truth. 'There's this girl in my class called Moji. She . . . she makes me do things for her.' Kuki couldn't look at him any more and stared at the ground as she spoke.

'What did she want you to get the money for, Kuki?' Dr D's voice was rising and she could hear the apprehension, the disbelief in it.

'Trainers,' she mumbled.

'What?'

'Trainers for her birthday,' she said louder. This time her voice broke and the dam holding back the tears broke as well. They spurted out and her shoulders shook with shame but also with anger at Moji and fear of what Dr D's reaction would be. He would be so disgusted and disappointed with her!

'I can't believe this! What kind of a useless' – Kuki cringed at every word he said. He was fuming! – 'wicked, devious brat would force someone to buy them a gift on their birthday!'

Kuki looked up in confusion and wiped her eyes with the back of her hand. He wasn't angry with her! He was furious about Moji.

'I will take you to school tomorrow and we'll go straight to the principal's office to clear the matter once and for all!'

'Would you actually do that? As in, go to school with me?' Kuki's eyes almost popped out of her head.

'Of course I will!' He suddenly looked uncertain. 'Is that not something that parents usually do? Not that I have any idea about these things. But we can't let that girl bully you around like that!' He scratched his head and looked uneasy. 'Normally I would leave this to your mum but there is no way we will bother her! This will remain between the two of us, OK?'

Kuki nodded quickly, very much happy to

agree with him on this point. Her mum would go up the wall if she found out.

'I'll have the principal set up a meeting with the parents of the girl, and you and the girl will be present, of course. And then we'll all have a very serious talk.'

Kuki suddenly imagined Moji's face, staring viciously at her. She almost choked in alarm and began to shake her head frantically. 'No . . . Dr D, I don't think that's a good idea. In fact, it would be awful and it would only make matters worse!'

'But you cannot tell me you want to go on like this? You can't be serious, Kuki. You can't just let people walk all over you. You have to assert yourself and say no even if you are afraid!'

Those were the same words Enilo had said to her, the day before. And Kuki knew Dr D and Enilo were both right.

She stared at the floor. Dr D's big feet seemed carelessly at ease around the place, while hers were small and awkward and neatly set in front of her. She wasn't like him. She wasn't like other people. It was easy for him to say things like this. It was easy for other people, other kids, to make friends, to boldly talk to others, say what they thought or felt. But it wasn't that way for her!

And yet when she thought of the past weeks since she'd started this new school, she realized for the first time in her life she didn't like what she had become. Even if she was shy and didn't have many friends and wasn't one of the popular kids, she had actually always still liked herself. She had never been ashamed of herself until now.

'Are you listening to me at all?' Dr D asked.

'Yes,' she said, in a small voice.

'I know it's easier said than done, but if you don't want me to clear the matter for you then I'll have to make you promise that you will! This week, OK?' He was looking at her intensely, waiting.

So even though her heart was beating against her ribcage as if it were trying to break through and the noise it was making inside of her was so loud she could hardly hear herself think, Kuki nodded vigorously.

Yes! She was going to put an end to it!

30

CLASS READING GONE VERY WRONG

Kuki left the house wanting to feel like a brave activist marching out to protest. But unfortunately she didn't feel brave. Her legs felt wobbly and thin, like they wouldn't even make it to school. And also she didn't have time to march resolutely because she was late. Instead she was running, panting and sweating.

The day had started all wrong. She had overslept. Of all days! They had English first thing and she had to give Moji her notebook and talk to her *before* the lesson started!

She had stayed up late, trying to work out how to write the essay for Moji. One very last, final homework for Moji. She had fiddled with the shell bracelet on her wrist, which Enilo had made for her. She had thought of her friend with pain and fear, but at the same time Enilo's words had spurred her on. She wanted to be brave and she wanted to stand up to Moji. After many versions and a lot of wasted paper, she had finally had an idea that had felt right. With gritted teeth and a thumping heart, she had whipped her pen across the page and written the biography with determined, decisive strokes. Then she had shoved the notebook into her bag, swearing that it would be the very last time, and zipped the bag closed.

Kuki managed to get to school and squeeze through the gates, in the very last minute before the teacher on duty closed them. The tall teacher, whom she didn't know, peered at her with two disapproving eyes from beneath one extra-long bushy eyebrow that went across his forehead. 'Hurry up now and next time a bit earlier! You don't want to start off your day with punishment, do you?'

Kuki rushed through the already empty corridors desperately hoping that Mr Akinte wouldn't be extra early. Her heart felt like it had moved up at least ten centimetres and was beating wildly in her throat. She pushed open the door of her classroom, wheezing like a broken air conditioner . . .

. . . and bumped directly into Moji.

'I was just about to go looking for you,' Moji hissed, holding out her hand.

Kuki glanced into the classroom. To her relief it was still rowdy. Mr Akinte had not yet arrived. She rummaged in her rucksack and pulled out the notebook.

Moji snatched it out of her trembling hands. 'And I can hardly wait for my gift. Even though you disappointed me yesterday by not coming to school and ruining my birthday. But I knew you would be a good puppy and deliver!'

Moji's words were wicked jabs as usual but strangely today they seemed less sharp. It was as if they bounced off an invisible shield. Kuki's talks with Dr D and Enilo seemed to have given her the courage.

In the row behind Moji she saw Faith watching them. Kuki took a deep breath, gathering her thoughts quickly to decide how to tell her.

'Number one, I am not your puppy,' she said.

'Number two, I am not giving you any gift because you are not my friend, and number three, I will not be doing your homework for you any more.' Kuki had said the words so fast that they had stumbled over each other on the way out of her mouth. She gulped but felt elated.

Moji's eyebrows creased. 'What do you mean?'

'I wrote you an essay, the last thing I will do for you, but it is just for you, not for submitting to Mr Akinte!' Kuki tried to make her voice sound firmer but it came out in jerks. She didn't care. She had managed to say everything, just as she had planned. She straightened her shoulders properly and looked Moji in the eyes.

Moji's face was a rapid contortion of surprise, shock, disappointment and anger all at the same time.

The door opened behind Kuki. 'Good morning, class! Everyone to their seats please!'

'We will talk afterwards,' Moji hissed. Then she bumped her sharp elbow into Kuki before hurrying to her seat. Kuki stumbled and hit her knee painfully against a desk.

'Careful now!' Mr Akinte called.

Kuki slipped into her seat feeling dizzy and worried.

'I hope everyone's day started off wonderfully! Mine definitely did!' Mr Akinte said in his ever-eager voice. Today he wore his red-and-yellow shirt with green palm trees on it. It made him look like a parrot as he strutted excitedly to the blackboard.

'Today I have decided we will have a reading session! Instead of you submitting your homework to me, I want you to read your biographies to the class. Isn't that a wonderful way for everyone to get to know their classmates better? You might find out the most brilliant things about each other, which you didn't know.' He grinned and clapped his hands excitedly.

A wave of groans went through the class and everyone began whispering and mumbling with their neighbours.

Kuki squirmed uneasily at the thought of reading about herself to the class.

'And I have decided that the grades for this essay are going to count double, so make sure you present yourselves loud and clearly and with a lot of enthusiasm.'

More groans came from around the class and Kuki immediately felt her belly tighten. Moji was going to be in more serious trouble than she had thought for not having her essay. Would she say she forgot it at home? She had often done that in the past.

'So who will start?' Mr Akinte glanced around. 'Moji, you are already holding your notebook, why don't you go ahead?'

Moji glanced nervously at Kuki as she opened her notebook. But then she discovered the essay and grinned with a self-righteous nod.

Kuki shook her head wildly. She tried to cough and gesture to Moji. Had she not understood? The essay was just for her! Not for the teacher! And definitely not for the entire class!

'Kuki! Will you behave yourself and stop disturbing the class! I am happy to see that you are so eager to read yours, but you will have to wait till I call you up.'

Some kids snickered at that and Kuki heard calls of oversabi and efiko. But she didn't even care. She just watched with horror as Moji began to read.

'My name is Moji Makinde. I am tall, slim, have a lovely smile and I am actually quite smart.'

Some snorts came from around the class.

Moji looked up and turned to Kuki with a smug smile.

'The problem is I do not believe in my . . . self . . .' Moji came to a stop and stared at the notebook. Kuki watched her gulp, her fingers tightening their grip on the page.

'Well, that was a brilliant start,' Mr Akinte said. 'Go on now, Moji, you definitely have our attention there!'

But Moji didn't react. She just sat there as still as a statue, staring at the page with a stony face.

'Faith, how about helping her read the essay.' Faith, whose desk was right beside Moji's, jerked up in surprise. 'Moji seems to be a bit shy to continue but she has us so interested now,' Mr Akinte said with twinkling, enthusiastic eyes.

Faith threw a worried glance at Moji and then at Kuki before reaching across to take the book out of Moji's hands. Faith looked extremely nervous, even scared as she had to literally tear the book out of Moji's grasp.

Kuki swallowed, her mind in turmoil. This was definitely not how she had imagined this. Should she just run away and escape? Tell her mum to put her in another school? Or should she grab the notebook, tear out the page, chew it up and run?

But it was too late. Faith began reading and the entire class was as silent as the assembly hall when the principal was in a bad mood.

'My biggest problem is that I do not have a single strand of self-confidence in me,' Faith read, her voice loud and clear but slightly shaky.

Someone from behind class snickered quietly, but everyone else seemed too interested to even make a sound.

Faith glanced uncomfortably at Moji before continuing. 'But I have become an expert in hiding this fact. I am a fake, a wannabe. The most important thing to me is what people think of me. I don't think anything of myself, so what others think of me is important. I would do anything, go to any lengths, just to have people think I am cool. Even if it means lying, cheating or being unkind to others.

'This is very unfortunate because actually I

have some good traits, but I would never show them. I could probably smile if I wanted to but I prefer to sneer or scowl and I am sure I could actually be a funny person, but I definitely prefer to use my humour to make fun of others or bring them down, rather than make people happy.

'I could have better grades, if I wanted to, but I am extremely lazy and I don't believe in myself anyway. So rather than work hard and show my good sides, I prefer to cheat, bully others into doing things for me and into telling me how wonderful I am even though I do not deserve it.'

Faith finished and there was a long awkward silence.

Kuki raised her head to glance at Moji. She seemed to have become smaller in her seat and Kuki's belly jolted at the sight of a large wet teardrop that fell on to Moji's desk.

'Well . . .' Mr Akinte said, and cleared his throat. 'I must say I have never heard such an honest, self-analysing piece in my entire career. Hmm . . .' He scratched his head, while studying Moji, obviously not sure how to assess the situation because she looked so miserable. 'Any comments?'

he asked the class with a nervous smile.

'I definitely would not have written that about myself,' Sahid ventured.

'I wouldn't give a five-star rating for that one, sha,' Joe called. Some kids laughed.

Moji got up suddenly, pushing her chair back into the desk behind hers with a loud crash. She took a few steps in Kuki's direction, her eyes red and her nostrils flared with anger.

'You back-stabbing, phoney, snake in the grass amebo!' she hissed.

'Now, now . . . what in heaven's name is going on here?' Kuki heard Mr Akinte call. But he sounded very far away and Kuki felt like roots had grown out of the ground and tied her to her seat, numbing her.

Moji took another step towards Kuki, stumbled over a rucksack and fell. The entire class roared with laughter. But Kuki wasn't finding any of this funny. She was shocked and couldn't believe what had just happened. Moji got up, her face wet with tears, and ran out of the classroom.

All eyes turned to Kuki for an explanation.

31

MORE WRONG DECISIONS

'Kuki, do you have anything to do with that essay?' Mr Akinte asked. He looked even more confused now and was beginning to sound very impatient.

There was a lot of whispering going on in class.

'Silence!' Mr Akinte called and turned back to Kuki, his face grim.

Kuki gulped before whispering. 'I'm sorry, sir, I need to go to the bathroom very badly.' And without waiting for permission, she rushed out of class too.

'Come back here! I will not tolerate this behaviour,' Mr Akinte called. His voice did not sound at all bright any more.

Kuki darted down the corridor; her belly was a double-knot and she was choking in an attempt not to cry. What was she doing? This was not her! Disobeying a teacher, running away from class!

She turned the corner and slammed into a small, soft barrier. Mrs Akerele.

'Goodness, what is this? Watch where you are going, girl! What is wrong with you? And what are you wearing there? Kuki, don't you know the rules? Students are only allowed to wear studs or small rings in school.'

Kuki touched her ears, realizing that she had forgotten to take Aunty's earrings out, the night before.

'I wouldn't have expected this of you, Kuki. Why are you not in class anyway?' Mrs Akerele was saying.

But Kuki wasn't listening. She just wanted to run from her, away from everyone. She could hardly believe what she was doing but she just darted past Mrs Akerele and ran.

'Come back here,' she heard Mrs Akerele call. 'This will have consequences.'

But Kuki ran and ran through the long

corridors. Where could she hide? She couldn't go to the bathrooms. She might meet Moji there, and meeting her alone now was the last thing she wanted!

She ran out of the building, not believing what she was doing. Had she actually just run away from two teachers? Like for real? She was going to get into the worst trouble ever! She ducked her head out of sight of the classroom windows and scurried close to the wall, around the building. Panting, she crept across the back lawn towards the sport hall, because she had remembered the boys in her class talking about seeing some seniors slip through the fence there to skip classes.

She remembered her shocked look on hearing that. She would never have believed it if someone had told her that a few weeks later she would find herself doing the same thing.

She ran all the way home.

It was only when she got to number fourteen that she realized to her dismay that she had left her bag in school with her mobile phone and house keys in it. She kicked the gate and would have screamed out loud if she hadn't worried that a neighbour might look out of a window and ask what she was doing there. She slumped down in the shade of the palm tree beside their gate, feeling absolutely miserable. When had her boring, uneventful life become so filled with trouble? Had she really just dumped school? Her belly folded and knotted itself rhythmically and painfully at the realization of what she had done. She was done for. And this was after she had just promised Dr D that she would get her act together and not do anything that would bother her mum!

After a while, she got up, and walked out of the estate and towards the busier main streets.

'Roasted corn! Delicious roasted sweet corn!' called the seller at the corner. She was fanning bright-orange cobs of corn with a piece of carton and eyed Kuki curiously as she called. Kuki hurried on, feeling like everyone knew she had ditched school. She felt all eyes on her as she passed. Parading around the city in her school uniform might not have been the best idea after all.

'Fine dress for fine girl,' a young man called from his street shop. He was holding up a bright-green dress with glittering sequins and waving it in her direction. His loudspeakers were blasting afrobeats into the street so loudly that he had to shout to make himself heard. His voice was rough from shouting. He waved the dress again.

Kuki shook her head and lurched forward to escape. She almost hit a young boy about her age who was carrying a heavy-looking tray on his head. His eyes widened in shock as he steadied the tray, just managing to stop the cans of soft drinks from falling off.

'Sorry,' she mumbled.

He just ignored her and continued calling 'pure wotaaa!' to the cars on the street.

Kuki spotted the mall ahead, and rushed in. Maybe she could find a corner to hide there. And it would be cooler in the air-conditioned shops. Soon she was eyeing snacks and fast-food stands as she gradually grew hungry. But she had no money with her, so all she could do was fill her belly with the scent of fries, burgers and spicy chicken as she wandered around.

When she caught sight of a homeless woman and her daughter begging at the entrance of the mall her thoughts immediately wandered to Enilo.

Her heart went out to her friend and she wished she could help her somehow. She missed her, terribly. Enilo was the only one she could talk to. But after her shocked look the day before, the way she had disappeared from her room once again, Kuki wondered if she could still count on Enilo being her friend. She had looked like she never ever wanted to have anything to do with her again.

She had to convince her that she was fine! That she was not possessed and not going to die any minute. There had been pain in Enilo's eyes. Kuki had seen it. And disgust. And fear. She sighed. What if Enilo never came back? The thought of losing her only friend suddenly made her feel so ill that she stopped in her tracks. No! She had to do something! Swiftly, she left the mall, her feet carrying her with long, determined strides.

32

A SIESTA THAT
LASTED TOO LONG

The house of shells stood in front of her like an ancient, graceful phantom. Like a faded photo of a grand house taken once-upon-a-time in a lost, quiet moment. Too quiet. Every step that Kuki took on the gravel path was like a loud announcement of her approach. Her intrusion.

She stopped in her tracks shortly before she reached the house and stared at it. Was she really sure about this? She remembered Enilo tugging her arm the evening before, running as if spirits had been chasing them. But surely there had been nothing? She had been here three times already – this would be her fourth visit. Every time, the house had evoked the strangest feelings in her. But wasn't it just the simple fact that it was so different, so dilapidated and elegant, and so out of place in the middle of nowhere? But really it was just an old mansion, its walls creaking and weighed down by dust and age and maybe some sad memories. There was no need to be superstitious just because Enilo had said it was haunted.

Kuki scanned the dirty panes of the windows uneasily, looking for any signs of movement or strangeness. But there was nothing unusual. Just the palm trees rustling their spiky leaves quietly in the nearly windless afternoon.

She drew a short, determined breath and shook her head. She didn't believe in any spirits and she didn't want to hear or think about the word 'Abiku', ever again in her life! And anyway Enilo had said the house of shells was only dangerous at night. This was crashing-hot daylight and the only things that were in the slightest way close to scary were the fat orange-headed lizards climbing up the walls and nodding their heads between every step.

Kuki continued towards the house but tried to tread as quietly as she could. She didn't call Enilo's name. She sneaked in quietly through the door and listened. Nothing. She went straight through to the blue-tiled courtyard.

The gnarled tree gleamed silvery in the shimmering sunlight, stretching its branches into all corners of the yard as if to force away all doubt that it was the rightful owner of this space. But it looked as normal as any old tree should look, and Kuki wondered what the strange light of dusk had done the evening before to jumble up her mind. She walked to the tree and peered around it, at the spot where she had found Enilo the first time. But she was nowhere to be seen.

The tree was a perfect umbrella from the burning hairdryer feel of the sun overhead. But the minute she leant against its rough trunk she was overcome by a sudden feeling of dizziness and nausea. It was so overwhelming that she had to lean her entire weight against the tree to stay upright. It almost felt like gravity's pull had suddenly grown stronger, making her feel drowsy. A sharp scent of leaves and bitter herbs filled her nose and she looked up into the silvery darkness of the tree's crown. The dark spaces between the leaves were like a maze and seemed to go on and on until they disappeared into a deeper darkness behind. The tree did not let a single ray of sunlight through, even though from the outside it had looked more like a swirling head of gnarled branches rather than a thick-leaved crown.

Kuki struggled to keep standing. A dreadful chill gripped her and she felt terribly cold and tired. She stumbled back into the house and began climbing the stairs. It was as if her body realized from one moment to the next that the few hours of sleep she had had, because of staying up to write Moji's biography, were absolutely not enough. Her limbs felt heavy and slow, like she was pulling them through water. Her eyes were drooping.

'Enilo? Are you up here?' Her voice was so quiet that she wondered if she had only imagined speaking aloud.

Just a little nap, she thought weakly, and then fell on to the dirty grey sheet covering the large four-poster bed. Dust made her sneeze and a mouldy smell filled her nostrils.

And then, she fell into a deep and overpowering sleep.

33

THE TRUTH
ABOUT ENILO

When Kuki woke up she didn't know where she was. She peered around in the darkness, trying to recognize the familiar structures of her shelf and desk. She had a very unsettling feeling that there was something very important that she should be thinking about, but she could absolutely not remember what it was.

She groped around and was surprised to find her fingertips touching a tall, hard post at the foot of the bed. It was when she realized it was a wooden bedpost that it all came back. She wasn't at home! This was not her room. She had ditched school, come looking for Enilo and fallen asleep.

Oh no! It was late. Her mum. She hadn't left a

message, didn't have her phone!

Kuki jumped off the bed and groped her way to the door in panic. How could she have stayed out so late! Now she had made things even worse. What was she going to say? What was her excuse for all this?

She had to get out of the house. There was definitely something odd about it. Every single time she had come here, she had ended up being late! As if it caught her in its spell and tried to keep her.

She hurried down the stairs in the gloomy hallway. Halfway she stopped abruptly. She had heard something.

An even more scary thought hit her. She was in the old, haunted house and it was night! *You should never be here at night*, Enilo had said. She gulped in fright and even though she felt like running away faster than ever, she tiptoed down as slowly and quietly as possible.

Now she heard it again. Chattering voices! It had come from outside. Her heart began to race. They seemed to be coming from the backyard. When she reached the landing she heard laughter. It sounded carefree and childish and she stood there for a brief second, listening. Then she heard Enilo's voice. But though it was loud and clear and firm, Kuki sensed something was wrong.

'Leave me alone,' Enilo said.

There was giggling and jeering.

'No, I am tired of your games!' Enilo shouted.

Kuki crept hurriedly through the mirrored room. If Enilo needed help, then she couldn't leave her alone.

She peered outside. It was lighter than within the mansion. Moonlight spread its rays across the tree in a smoky kind of fog and the silvery branches reflected it across the yard. The blue tiles made it seem as if the tree had grown out of a silvery-blue lake. Its crown quivered strangely in the moonlight like the night before, and with a start Kuki realized that there were bodies in the trees. The silhouettes of children moving from one branch to another. There was something odd about them that Kuki could not explain. They were skinny and ragged but at the same time their dark skin seemed to glow in the moonlight. They moved about the branches with such ease and elegance that the crown of the tree looked like a writhing mass.

Kuki's eyes felt as if they were burning from shock.

Enilo stood beneath the tree looking up. She looked tiny.

Suddenly something glided off a branch and landed smoothly in front of Enilo. Arms, legs, a body and a face formed out of the shadows. Eyes glowing strangely red narrowed.

'You think you are better than us. You and your friend? You think she is your friend, but she is not!'

Enilo took a slow step backwards as the boy towered above her, shoulders arched forward.

Kuki grasped the door frame tightly as she watched them.

'Sooner or later, you will give in. You will succumb and end it. And do you know why?' His eyes glowed even redder and Kuki blinked, unsure if her sight was blurred. But the red eyes remained focused on Enilo and the boy continued in a harsh, sneering tone, 'Because it is in your nature!'

'No!' Enilo cried angrily. 'Never! I will not.'

She turned and marched away from the boy, towards the house. Towards Kuki.

Kuki's heart skipped a beat. She stumbled backwards, not wanting Enilo to discover her.

She almost fell in her haste to escape and as she scrambled away as quietly as possible, she tried to get her head around what she had seen. There was something wrong with the children in the tree. There was something wrong with Enilo.

'You cannot run from that which is part of you. You cannot run from yourself!' she heard the boy call. Then loud chatter and giggling and other voices repeating in unison, 'You cannot run from yourself.'

It felt like the voices were speaking to her and even though they were not, Kuki allowed the words to touch her, to enter her.

'*You cannot run from yourself.*'

And as they sank into her every pore she finally allowed herself to fully realize what she had seen. The truth about Enilo. And about herself! The truth that she had known all along. Her entire life. That she, bearer of the name Kokumo, had spent her life running a hopelessly pointless race. A race away from herself and from the truth.

Hot tears burnt her cheeks as she pushed open the tall front door. She cringed when it made a ghostly creaking sound. Enilo and the others must have heard it! She glanced back, but in the darkness could not see anyone behind her. She rushed through the doorway. Outside she stopped abruptly.

Enilo was standing in front of her.

Her eyes were piercing in the moonlight. And glowing fiery red.

34

THE THREAT FROM THE OUTSIDE

'How did you get here so quickly?' Kuki was seething with hot anger that she could hardly contain. Even as the words left her lips, she realized that that wasn't what she really wanted to know.

So when Enilo didn't reply, she asked: 'I thought you were my friend?' Her voice was strange to her ears. It sounded harsh and broken.

'I am your friend . . .' Enilo began.

'No!' Kuki shook her head furiously. She didn't know what Enilo was, but she was definitely not her friend! She had deceived her all this while. And Kuki had been foolishly living a lie for weeks. For her entire life!

'I would never hurt you, Kuki,' Enilo said in a sharp whisper.

'It is in your nature! Have you forgotten? Isn't that what your friend back there told you?'

'Shh,' Enilo hissed with a nervous look behind Kuki. 'Don't let them hear you. They mustn't know you are here!'

'Cold and heartless is what the Abiku are! That's what you told me. Only then I didn't know that you were talking about yourself!' Kuki spat the words at her, her mouth tasting bitter and dry. 'That was when I still thought you were on my side!'

Enilo's red eyes flashed angrily and she shook her head. Her chest was heaving and she was obviously fighting to keep calm.

'Your very existence is my downfall,' Kuki continued, her voice breaking. Her words weighed her down. The realization of what all this meant for her was too much to bear. 'I wish I had never met you.'

Enilo's face contorted and took on a ghastly look. She grabbed Kuki's arms and began to speak. But the words seemed to stick in her throat. A look of surprise and then pain twisted her face, and she hastily let go of Kuki as if she had been burnt.

Kuki watched her in confusion.

Enilo hunched forward, her hands on her knees and gasping for breath. 'Are you carrying a charm?'

Kuki stared at her but then, realizing what it was, her hands went up to the earrings Aunty had given her. She smiled. A tired, resigned tug of her lips. To think that Aunty had been right all this while. She had really only wanted to protect her.

'I can't believe I am actually possessed, like Aunty warned me,' she said. 'I thought I was supposed to be watching out for myself on the inside. I didn't know the threat was there already. From the outside. From the one person I would least have expected it. From a friend!' Kuki marched past Enilo. 'Keep away from me!' she cried when she heard steps following her. 'Stay out of my life!'

Suddenly Enilo was standing in front of her again. She had materialized out of the thick night air, spreading her arms and blocking the gap in the gate.

'Let me go!' Kuki snarled. She was surprised at the venom in her own voice. 'And stay out of my life!'

'I can't!' Enilo hissed back at her, her eyes flaring up. 'Don't you understand? That's not how this works.'

The night suddenly thickened as clouds covered the moon and Enilo's shape melted into the darkness. All that Kuki could see now were two red dots of light hovering in front of her.

'I want you to get out of the way; if not I'll have to push you aside, and I don't think you want me to touch you right now!'

'No!' Enilo's voice hissed. 'We. Have. To. Talk!'

'I do not need you,' Kuki hissed back. 'Stay away! I don't ever want to see you again!' She tore the shell bracelet that Enilo had made for her off her wrist and threw it on the ground at Enilo's feet. Then she lunged forward, pushing Enilo's slight body out of the way. She heard a gasp of pain but she didn't turn back.

Not when the rusty gates rattled and screeched so furiously, she thought they would break.

Not when the shadows of the trees beside her flared up in a red angry burst. And not when an unearthly, angry wail split the eerie darkness.

35

A PROMISE THAT SHOULD NOT HAVE BEEN MADE

The lights in every room of house number fourteen were on. The door and gate stood wide open. Dr D was on the street in front of the house, speaking loudly into his phone, and her mum was talking agitatedly to the neighbours from the house opposite. Kuki knew immediately that she was in very, very big trouble.

She ran forward, calling, 'I'm here, Mum! I'm fine! Sorry I'm late.'

Her mum let out a half-wail and grabbed her into a hug.

'I told you, it was much too early to be

worried,' one of the neighbours said. 'Kids nowadays are like that. So carefree.'

'Oh, she just came back,' Dr D said into his phone. 'Thank you very much for your time, so sorry for bothering you.' He switched off his phone and then he shook hands with the neighbours. 'So sorry to bother you all,' he mumbled.

Her mum didn't even say a word. She just walked in to the house, and slumped on to the sofa, elbows balanced on her huge belly and her face in her hands.

'I can't believe you would do this, Kuki!' Dr D said, his voice drawn tight. 'Your school called to say you actually ran off! In the middle of the lesson! And then you disappear, don't pick up your calls and stay away for hours, even after dark. I must say I am shocked! Your mum and I had the most worrisome afternoon!'

He glared at Kuki and Kuki swallowed nervously.

'I thought we agreed just yesterday that we didn't want to bother your mum?'

Kuki glanced at her mum. She knew deep down somewhere she should feel sorry for worrying them, but as Dr D spoke she felt too far away from what was happening. Her thoughts were still at the house of shells. Her thoughts hovered around a writhing tree, silvery and eerie in the moonlight, around dark undefined limbs, red glowing eyes and wicked laughter. Around a girl whom she had trusted and thought was her friend. The word 'Abiku' echoed again and again in her head. At first a thin snickering whisper, but then louder and threatening, quicker and quicker like a song exploding and reaching its dramatic climax.

Kuki covered her ears and screamed. A terrible pain shot through her body and then she was falling.

Whispers around her brought her slowly back to the reality of her room and her bed.

'Are you feeling better now, Kuki?'

Kuki focused out of the blur. Worried faces, foreheads lined with ridges and furrows, lips pressed together tightly and fists clasping and unfolding.

'Kuki, sweetheart, you fainted,' her mum said.

'Are you OK?'

'I didn't eat or drink anything all day, that's all,' Kuki mumbled, her voice croaky and dry.

'Oh, that explains the fainting. She is dehydrated!' Dr D said, and hurried out of the room. 'I'll get her a glass of water,' he called.

Kuki closed her eyes. She still felt weak and dizzy. But most of all she felt angry. She was fed up of worried faces, of pretending to be fine even though she was not. She felt like bawling loudly for at least two hours to let everything she felt out.

'Here you are,' Dr D said, returning with a glass. 'Drink something and you will soon feel better.'

'And what if I don't feel better?' she spat out, surprised again at the viciousness in her croaky voice. 'Then what?'

'Hey, calm down now, Kuki,' Dr D warned.

'Well, maybe we should all get used to the fact that I might possibly not be OK once in a while!'

'What are you talking about?' her mum cried, looking confused.

'I thought you were so sure that I wasn't an Abiku child? If you are so sure, then being ill shouldn't be a problem, right? That shouldn't have you worried, right? Because I'm tired of being the perfectly healthy and happy child, just so you won't worry, Mum!'

'Kuki! That's enough!' Dr D cried.

Her mum stared at her, her mouth half open, but no words came out. Her eyes were full of pain.

Kuki didn't even understand why she was so mad at her mum. Why was she being so mean to her? 'Kuki, is that how you feel?' her mum asked quietly.

Kuki avoided her eyes. She had absolutely no idea how she felt, right now.

'I'm so sorry, honey, I didn't know that! I don't want you to worry about me! I am perfectly fine. And like I have told you a hundred times before, I know for sure, one hundred per cent, that Abikus do not exist. I wish you would finally also believe this and stop worrying about it! You are not an Abiku child and nothing will happen to you!'

Kuki snorted, turned her back to them and closed her eyes, tears seeping into her pillow.

She suddenly knew why she was so mad at her

mum. All this time, she had made her feel safe.
She had promised her that Abiku didn't exist.

But they did exist!

And there was one in their very own house.

36

A WORD WITH
MR AKINTE

'Conniving to partake in an act of deception in which you wilfully tried to trick your teacher! Otherwise known as fraud!' Mr Akinte counted one finger on his left hand.

Kuki drummed her fingers steadily into her palms. It was Monday – after her faint, her mum had kept her off school at the end of the previous week, but now she was back, and facing the music for her behaviour. They were sitting at his desk in a corner of the staffroom, surrounded by the low hum of the few teachers who had not yet gone to their classes. But she felt distant. Her life was the biggest mess at the moment. This was the smallest of her problems. She was becoming good at taking the shocks that her life was obviously so eager to dish out to her at the moment.

'Submitting your work under someone else's name, otherwise known as plagiarism.' He counted another finger.

'Running out of class and away from school, deliberately disobeying teachers who were calling you back! Otherwise known as insubordination!' He raised a third, final finger.

'We do not tolerate such behaviour in this school!' He looked at her sternly and she tried to hold his gaze briefly before looking back down at her hands.

Mr Akinte leant back in his chair, his silky yellow-and-grey striped shirt tightening around his belly as he did so. 'You are lucky that until now you have been a well-behaved student without any past records.'

Kuki nodded and realized she was relieved to see his face softening a little.

'Faith told me that Moji had been very nasty to you, forcing you to do her homework for her, among other things.'

Kuki's eyes widened as she stared at him. Faith

had told him about Moji!

'You were a victim of bullying.'

Kuki nodded, feeling embarrassed.

'But the boldness of your strategy there, to actually cold-bloodedly allow your rival, your antagonist, to run into the knife!' Mr Akinte's eyes were suddenly bright and alive just like they always were in English class. 'The bully turned victim and made to be the reader of her own essay, the architect of her own downfall!' He spread out his arms, his eyes mischievous and staring into the distance as if he were an actor in a theatre.

Kuki shook her head. 'No, Mr Akinte! It wasn't like that! I really didn't want that for her. I told her the essay wasn't meant for anyone else. Just for her!'

But he wasn't listening. His body was tense, just like when he was analysing the meaning of Cyprian Ekwensi's or Chinua Achebe's words.

'The ingenuity of that!' he said and clapped his hands together. 'I can't help but admire that manoeuvre, Kuki. What a bold move!'

Kuki stared at him, now truly lost for words.

'But anyway,' he said rather abruptly, his concentration back on her. 'I had a very serious talk with Moji last week. We do not tolerate such antisocial behaviour in our students. We are a school of impeccable reputation and Moji was lucky not to have been suspended. She will write three essays for me on the topics of fraud, plagiarism and bullying respectively and she will face other consequences. In any case, she will not bother you any more. And if there is anything at all, even just one bad word from her, I want you to inform me about it with immediate effect!'

Kuki nodded slowly, already wondering what her own punishment would be.

'Now in the meantime I want you to see Mrs Akpan for counselling. Her counselling hours are Wednesdays after school. Understood?'

'Yes, sir,' Kuki whispered.

'OK, then. You are free to go. Here is your school bag which you left behind.' He handed it to her and gestured towards the door.

She stared at him in disbelief and confusion. 'Ehm . . .'

'That's all right! As I said, you are very lucky

that you are new to the school, your school record is spotless and your grades are very good. After speaking with Mrs Akpan we have decided to let you off the hook considering the circumstances. The condition, of course, is that such behaviour never occurs again!' He raised a final warning finger.

37

A VERY DIFFERENT KIND OF SCHOOL EXPERIENCE

When Kuki opened the classroom door, the first lesson had already begun. Everyone turned to stare at her. She quickly turned to the teacher.

'Please excuse me for being late, I was in a meeting with Mr Akinte,' she mumbled, her voice hoarse with worry.

'No problem, I was aware of your meeting, Kuki,' Mrs Jones said. 'Have a seat and open your workbook to page thirty-one.'

'Yes, ma!'

She stumbled through the row. Despite the days

off, she still felt bouts of weakness since her faint and she could feel one coming right now with all eyes on her. But strangely, there were a lot of friendly looks! She frowned, didn't watch her step and knocked against a desk leg. Her rucksack dropped out of her hands on to the floor. No one laughed as they usually would have done. Joe's hand shot out and he handed it to her. With a smile!

She glanced around quickly and saw that Moji was sitting in the last row, head bowed over her book. No one ever sat in the last row. She was all alone.

When the bell rang for break, Kuki had hardly closed her book when Faith appeared at her desk. She smiled shyly. 'Can I sit with you under the tree where you always sit at break time?'

Kuki stared at her, confused. Then she jerked round, to see if Moji was watching and if she would storm over to drag Faith from her. But Moji was sitting over her book like she had been earlier. Like she had not moved an inch in the past three hours.

Kuki shrugged. Why not?

'Don't forget your lunch,' Faith said and

headed out of the classroom.

Kuki grabbed her lunch box and hurried after her with another quick look at Moji. She seemed to be filling her page with hundreds of circles. Bunmi nodded at Kuki as they passed. She usually acted as if Kuki was a whiff of bad air whenever she saw her. Now she was nodding?

'Why is everyone acting so strangely?' Kuki asked Faith as soon as they were seated in her favourite spot, far away from all the groups of friends that gathered at break time. It was strange sitting here with someone and she still wasn't sure what to make of all this.

'You are a hero!' Faith said with a grin.

'Heh? I don't get it!'

'You stood up to Moji. You are the first person to have ever boldly said no to her. I mean you actually disgraced her in front of the entire class and made her the laughing stock! She was so ashamed; she hasn't spoken a word to anyone since. The boys have been throwing some wicked comments at her, saying hurtful things and she didn't even make any effort to fight back.'

'Oh!'

'I think she is kind of broken. Like she's lost all her pepper.'

'Oh!' was all Kuki could say. She hadn't actually planned for Moji to be the laughing stock of the class. She thought of how very dejected Moji had looked, drawing hundreds of circles on her jotter.

'Well, serves her right!' Kuki heard herself saying. 'She can't just go around bullying people into doing things for her.'

'Yeah, that's what I mean! You told her "no"! You are so brave!'

Kuki nodded, even though she had felt anything but brave; she had been scared stiff.

Faith was grinning widely but Kuki didn't feel like smiling back. She was sure it would make her cheeks hurt. She didn't feel at all comfortable with the situation and she didn't trust Faith, who had tried to be friendly but abandoned her and put her in even more trouble the moment Moji had appeared.

'So why is everyone gloating now?' she asked, feeling slightly disgusted. 'I thought you were her friends? Isn't it sneaky, how the moment your friend isn't cool any more, you all turn away from her, make fun of her and look for new friends?'

'It's not sneaky!' Faith cried, looking hurt. 'I didn't make fun of Moji, I only told you what the others did. Moji bossed all of us around, you know. We just all went along with her because we were afraid. Everyone wanted to be on good terms with her. No one wanted to end up being her victim, like—' She stopped talking and avoided Kuki's eyes.

'Like me?'

Faith didn't reply. 'We were cowards,' she said quietly. 'I'm sorry, Kuki. I always wanted to be your friend. I watched you writing under the tree during break time. And I always wanted to know what you were writing. I . . . I like writing stories and I have filled five diaries already with my ideas and some stories. But no one I know is interested in writing.'

'The reason I began writing under the tree was because no one wanted to hang out with me during break time! What else was I supposed to do?' Kuki cried.

Faith turned away and Kuki saw her eyes were actually brimming with tears. 'Just even looking at you or having a word with you got Moji angry.

I really never understood why she was so against you. She always said mean things about you. She said that you lived in a tiny old flat on the same street where her own house is. It was almost as if she was ashamed that you lived on the same street as her.'

'What? *She* is the one who lives in a flat on my street . . .'

Kuki's jaw dropped as she suddenly realized what Moji's problem was. Now it all made sense. Moji was ashamed of her home.

Kuki thought of Moji's old sandals and how she had tried on her trainers. Kuki had just been unlucky that she lived on the same street as Moji. All the bullying and keeping everyone in class away from her had just been to make sure it never came out where she lived!

'So you mean she made it all up? She was always trying to act all posh but I often found her fake,' Faith said. 'Though she could really be very convincing.'

Kuki sighed, feeling tired. All this just because Moji was ashamed. She wouldn't even have mentioned this fact to anyone. What was so special about living in a house or in a flat? It wasn't something she had ever dwelled upon and it didn't make a difference to her. Her best friend didn't even have a pair of shoes!

At that thought she felt a cold jab in her insides as she remembered that last horrible night. Goosebumps popped up on her skin.

Enilo was no longer her friend. She hadn't seen her now for four whole days!

There was an awkward silence. She knew Faith was waiting for her to respond. To agree to be friends.

Kuki clenched her fists angrily. Why couldn't things just be easy? What if she just stayed out of Enilo's way? If she could banish her from her life and forget the things she'd seen at the house of shells, maybe her life could turn for the better. She was thirteen now and safe from harm from any Abiku. She could be a normal girl with a normal friend sitting under a tree at break time. Yes, she was going to forget she had ever met Enilo!

'What do you like to write about?' she asked Faith in a determined voice.

38

A DANGEROUS PLAN

'Go away!'
'I can't!'

'I said I never want to see you again!' Kuki glared at Enilo who was gripping the curtain tightly with her thin fingers. This time she hadn't pretended to have come in through the window; she'd just appeared suddenly in the corner, giving Kuki a terrible fright. At least Enilo's eyes didn't have the horrible red glow of that night at the house of shells.

Kuki snatched up the book that had fallen out of her hands in shock, and pretended to continue reading. She had been lying in bed all afternoon trying to read while her thoughts had circled around her strange day at school.

'I have been thinking, and I have worked out a plan! But can you please put down that book and get rid of those earrings so I can breathe calmly and tell you about it?'

Kuki glared at her, not moving. She wanted her own plan of ignoring Enilo, banishing her from her life, to work. So she folded her arms across her chest, daring Enilo to try and make her do anything.

Enilo stood her ground, staring Kuki down with large, grave eyes. Kuki could already feel her plan slipping away fast like hot beach sand through burnt fingers.

She threw the book down and stomped out of her room. Everyone was at work and the house was quiet. She sighed as she took out the earrings and dropped them on the sideboard in the corridor. Slowly she walked back to her room.

'Those children you saw at the house . . .' Enilo began when she entered the room. 'They are mean and evil.'

Kuki raised an eyebrow. 'And you are not?'

'I . . . I am not like them, I swear. They go back . . . back to our spirit world whenever they want, without thinking, without caring what it does to the families here.

'All these years they have made fun of me, were mean to me, because I wouldn't follow them. Because I didn't want to hurt you. That never bothered me. I didn't care. But now they have started threatening me. They want to force me to return to our world, not only to visit but to stay . . .' Enilo was picking at the frayed edge of Kuki's blanket, avoiding her eyes.

Kuki gulped, feeling ill. 'I don't understand,' she said slowly. 'What do you mean by "all these years"? Not wanting to hurt me?'

Enilo did not reply immediately. 'Kuki, you know exactly what that means,' she said softly.

Kuki shook her head almost violently.

'I have always been here with you.'

Kuki continued shaking her head even though she was already feeling dizzy and ill. 'That's not possible!' she said. 'I would have known. Felt it.'

'No, you would not have felt it,' Enilo said. 'We are not allowed to make ourselves known. Ever!'

Kuki looked at her sharply and Enilo nodded quickly. 'I have risked terrible consequences by showing myself to you. I was so shocked when you went to the house of shells that first time. I had to show myself to you, to get you away from there and out of danger!'

Enilo was whispering fearfully and Kuki saw terror in her eyes.

'I tried to warn you, I told you it was dangerous and that you shouldn't be out there, especially at night, but you were so persistent. You kept coming back!'

Kuki thought back to the afternoon of her birthday. It was weird that she had walked all the way there, through the short stretches of forest alone. But the other times she had gone there, she had done so because she had wanted to spend time with Enilo. Because she'd been lonely and didn't have any friends. Because she'd been worried about Enilo. That's why she hadn't cared about Enilo's warnings. She hadn't believed in spirits and haunted houses.

'I think moving here to Dr D's place, so close to the tree, caused some kind of connection between you and the house of shells.'

'What do you mean?' Kuki asked.

'The tree. It is the door to our world. That's where the Abiku who are in the human world meet every day at dusk. The tree is very powerful.'

Kuki shivered as she remembered how ill she had felt when standing beneath the eerie tree. And how the tree had been writhing with limbs.

'Some of the Abiku slip back into the spirit world at night to play with other Abiku there,' Enilo continued. 'They don't care that leaving the human world to play in the spirit world for just a few minutes makes their human child, the one they possessed, terribly ill. Like I told you, they are wicked and heartless.'

They both fell silent and Kuki allowed what she had just heard to sink in.

'So the other Abiku are trying to make you go back?'

Enilo nodded, shoulders sagging. 'The spirit world is calling me too. I can feel its call in my bones, every night at dusk. And the feeling has been growing stronger every night – I can hardly fight it any more.'

Kuki shook her head. This was all too much. Too weird. Too scary. She folded her arms across her chest. 'I don't even believe in you. You don't even exist!'

Enilo looked at her sadly. 'And yet here I am standing in front of you, am I not?' she asked quietly.

'But this all doesn't make sense. I am safe now! The Abiku myth says once a child reaches the age of thirteen, it is out of danger. I am thirteen already. That's the proof that I was never even possessed! I made it.'

Enilo shook her head sadly.

'But I am thirteen!' Kuki yelled in frustration.

'Not exactly,' Enilo said.

'What?'

'Do you remember that when you were a baby you were so ill that the doctors brought you to this world three weeks early?'

Kuki felt her heart begin to thud faster. Her mum had told her this. But how did Enilo know? She had never told her. Her belly flopped at the realization that if Enilo had always been part of her, then she knew everything about her.

Kuki sighed. 'And what does that mean?'

'It means your real birthday, the day you would

have come into this world of your own free will because you were ready to be born, that day is . . . today.'

'Today?' Kuki realized it was true. Her birthday, the day she had met Enilo for the first time at the house of shells, was exactly three weeks ago.

Enilo nodded. 'Today, the call of my world will be at its strongest, because it is the night of your *real* thirteenth birthday. The very last day in which I am allowed to stay with you. I have managed to resist for so long, but tonight will be tough. And the Abiku have warned me already that they will not let me come back.'

Enilo looked just as dejected as Kuki was feeling.

'But you managed to resist up till now. You never went back like the others.'

Enilo stared down at her hands, twisting them nervously. 'I did . . . long ago. That time when you fainted, when you were six.' She looked up now. 'I am so sorry that happened. I . . . was weak and I gave in to the call.'

Kuki shook her head. 'That's long past and forgotten,' she said.

'And at the house last week, after you left.' Enilo's voice was a tiny whisper. 'I don't know how it happened. I was so mad at you. The other Abikus dared me to go through, saying I was too attached and couldn't. I just did it. I'm so sorry. It was foolish, especially because the other Abiku could have tried to keep me there. But the moment I entered our world, I realized what I was doing and ran back. I was only gone for a few seconds. I hope it didn't hurt you too badly?'

Kuki stared at her for a long time, not saying anything. She wasn't even angry. Just confused. It was almost too much to understand: the connection between them, how closely tied her life was to Enilo and how completely dependent and vulnerable that made her. It was the most terrifying thing. But when she looked at Enilo, kneading her fingers and nervously crossing and uncrossing her thin legs, she felt hope. Somewhere inside her, she knew she could trust Enilo.

'Let's just forget it.'

Enilo leant forward slowly, looking shy. She held out something on her palm. Kuki glimpsed the bracelet that she had flung back at Enilo on that awful night. She took it, slipping it on. She had missed it. She had missed Enilo.

Kuki held out her little finger to Enilo. 'Friends?' she asked.

Enilo slipped her own little finger into Kuki's. 'Kindred spirits for ever,' she replied, in her whispery voice.

Kuki smiled and took a deep breath. 'OK, the important question is: what is going to happen now?'

Enilo's face turned serious.

Kuki held her breath, afraid of what she would hear.

'There is something special that every Abiku has. A precious token that binds us to our world. It is buried back home.' Enilo was whispering again. 'Mine is a good-luck shell. I buried it under the roots of a tree, near the water, in a place only I know. Every Abiku has their own special token and a secret hiding place for it. There is an old myth, a secret and dangerous song that has been whispered since for ever in the quiet shadows of our world. The whispers say that if an Abiku ever succeeds in taking their token out of the spirit world, then they can break their connection to the world for ever.'

'Oh, but that's perfect!' Kuki said, breathing out with relief. 'Why have you not done that?' But her excitement faded when she saw the look on Enilo's face.

'It's not that easy.'

Kuki sighed. There was obviously a catch.

'There are two problems. First of all, no one has ever tried to do this before, because it is dangerous. The whispers say that taking the token out of the spirit world is such an abomination that it will cause something too terrible to even imagine. Some say it would be the death of the Abiku. Some say it will close the door for ever. The whispers say that the Abiku cannot survive cutting the connection to the spirit world. But no one knows if this is true because no one has ever been so reckless.'

Enilo turned her face away to stare into the distance. She drew a long breath and closed her eyes. And then she began to sing in her eerie whispery voice.

Eku kpiti kpom kpom, eku kpiti kpo
Spirits come and spirits go
What is buried must never show
For only one must ever see
The sacred thing, beneath the deep

Eku kpiti kpom kpom, eku kpiti kpi
Spirits fierce and spirits mean
What is buried must never leave
If anyone should try to steal
The end of the road, the end it will be

When Enilo finished, she sighed. 'The problem is that other Abiku will be very watchful. They know that I am not happy. The whispers say that the token can only be removed on the night of the thirteenth birthday. So the other Abiku might guess what I want to do.'

Kuki felt her belly begin to twist painfully. The situation was beginning to sound hopeless.

But Enilo's face took on a determined look. 'I have to do this, Kuki! I have to go back one last time. Today, your true birthday, is our last chance! If I succeed, if I can return with my token, then I never need to go back ever again. I would be free and you would be safe.' She looked at Kuki now. Her eyes were hard and tense. 'I will need your help.'

'My help? What can I do?' Kuki asked, sitting up. She was ready to do anything if it meant she could end this nightmare.

'The tree is the door to the spirit world. But every evening as soon as it is dark the other Abiku meet there, some waiting to slip through the door to enter our world. To enter unnoticed and alone, I need you to lure them away from the tree.'

Kuki gasped. 'You want me to show myself to those evil spirits?'

Enilo nodded, looking very unhappy.

'How will that work?'

'I don't know. I guess the fact that you are there at our sacred place may be enough to make them wild with anger and make them chase you.'

'To make them wild with anger? And chase me? Are you joking?' Kuki cried. 'I don't want anyone chasing me. Let alone evil spirit children who are wild with anger! And there were so many of them, I'd be dead in a minute.'

'They can't hurt you if you wear protective charms like your earrings. And there are more charms in this house. I felt it in your parents' bedroom, under the bed.'

Kuki remembered Enilo breaking down in the bedroom that day and she shuddered at the memory. And when she thought of the night at the house of shells, the creepy Abiku slithering around on the tree and Enilo's red eyes glaring at her, she panicked.

'Why should I do that? Why should I risk my life?' Kuki closed her eyes and shook her head, not caring that she looked like a four-year-old.

'Kuki, we don't have *time*. I know this is a lot for you, but you have to understand what it means if they force me to go back and if they do not let me return. The moment I leave this world, you will fall ill. And if I do not return before midnight, then you—' She stopped, obviously afraid to finish. Enilo swallowed and stared at her, her lips trembling.

'I will die . . .' Kuki whispered.

39

THE LAST
HEART CRUMB

Enilo watched from a safe distance in the back-yard while Kuki dug around in the bins, wrinkling her nose in disgust. Finally, Kuki found what she had been looking for and triumphantly held up the smelly plastic bag her mum had thrown out. She tore open the bag eagerly and the charms, bangles and chains with tiny bells fell on the ground with a tinkle. Enilo covered her ears and shuddered.

Kuki got rid of the bag and washed her hands under the tap in the yard.

'Did you get into trouble last week after you came back from the house?' Enilo asked. 'Was Mum very worried?'

Enilo looked genuinely concerned and Kuki suddenly realized why she had felt so close to Enilo and made friends with her so naturally. Enilo knew everything about her. She knew her fears and the things she liked. She was a part of her.

'Are we the same?' she asked Enilo awkwardly.

Enilo shrugged. 'In a way, yes. But not in everything. We share the same experiences, so that makes us similar. Obviously as part of you I read all the books you read along with you and I've been to all the places you went. But we are also different in many things.'

'Like what?'

Enilo paused, thinking. 'I love scary books about ghosts and spirits,' she grinned. 'I was so disappointed when you didn't read the ghost books you bought.'

Kuki's head snapped up. She pointed at Enilo. 'It was you! *You* made me buy them!'

'Possibly,' Enilo replied, laughing.

'Every time I bought them, I wondered afterwards what made me do such a thing!'

They grinned at each other.

'Why didn't you help me become a more out-going person? Less shy and weird,' Kuki asked.

'I can't actually make you do things you don't want to. Don't forget I couldn't make you read the scary books. My longing was only enough to nudge you towards buying them, but not enough to make you actually read them. I can't change you or your character, Kuki. I can't fight your fights for you. All these things you have to do yourself.'

Kuki swallowed, feeling small and alone.

'You shouldn't care what others think. You are a good person. You have a big heart and you would never hurt anyone. You feel sorry even for people who are mean to you. That is a gift. A talent. You are special, Kuki.'

Kuki shook her head. 'I am so awkward around people and—'

'You are the best person I have shared a life with,' Enilo said, sharply. 'It was *you* who made me want to be good, not heartless! You made me want to hold on to my last heart crumb.'

Kuki lowered her gaze, now feeling shy. Not knowing what to say. And she wondered at the strangeness of sharing your body, your spirit, with someone else.

'How does it feel? I mean, inside of me? Is it not weird?'

'I have never known anything else. Abiku are parasites.' Enilo's lips twisted as she spat out the word. 'We live other people's lives. Feeding off their lives and then leaving them to die.' Then her face brightened. 'Sometimes I imagine myself being a pearl in an oyster. Oysters are amazing you know. They are one of the earliest forms of animal life and have existed for over half a million years. Do you know what they do when a parasite invades their shell?'

Kuki shook her head.

'They protect themselves by coating the parasite over and over with a beautiful substance they can produce, until it is shiny and beautiful and harmless. They turn the parasite into a pearl! And then they just go on living side by side with the precious pearl inside their shell. Isn't that wonderful?'

Kuki watched Enilo's eyes glow and she felt immensely sad for her.

'But you said your world is beautiful too? In

your world at least, you have a life? A family? Or friends?'

'How can I feel at home in a place that is beautiful but evil? How can I be friends with creatures who have no hearts?' Enilo's eyes blurred with angry tears.

'I am sorry to hear that, Enilo,' Kuki said sadly.

'In your world, Kuki, there is warmth and there is joy. And do you know where it all comes from?'

Kuki shook her head.

'From your hearts. Hearts filled with crumbs of kindness, crumbs of goodness.'

'But our world is not perfect, either,' Kuki said, trying to make her feel better. 'There is also a lot of hate and wickedness here.'

'Yes, but yet the good shines through. In every human heart there are crumbs of goodness, so at least there is a chance of kindness. Humans just need reminders once in a while and most of the time, the good works its way through.' Enilo sighed wistfully. 'I have lived many lives before this one and I hated myself in each one. Each life took away something from me.' She patted her chest sadly. 'There is just one last crumb left in my heart and if I don't make it back on time . . . if I don't succeed with our plan . . .'

Enilo didn't finish her sentence but Kuki knew exactly what she wasn't saying.

If they didn't succeed, then Enilo would lose her last heart crumb, and she would become heartless, like the others.

40

SHORTLY BEFORE MIDNIGHT

Kuki opened her window quietly and glanced out. There had been a power cut and the street was in complete darkness, allowing the night to show its true face.

The sky was covered by a curtain of clouds and only a slight yellowing in one spot gave an idea of where the moon might be hidden. The darkness left just enough light and shadow to make everything look like a potential monster. The trees looked like long skinny hands clawing at the sky. The houses in the estate like a crowd of shrouded ghosts huddled against each other for support.

A cold fear gripped Kuki.

It was a night in which you wouldn't even want

to put your head outside your window, let alone walk your entire body to an abandoned building infested by wicked spirit children.

Kuki shuddered and closed the window quietly. She picked up her torch and the charms, which she had wrapped in a small cloth, and left her room. She had gone to bed fully dressed in jeans and a T-shirt and even her trainers, and she would leave the house at eleven on the dot as planned. Earlier would have been better but they had been worried that Kuki might get caught sneaking out and then all would have been lost.

The house was as quiet and as tense as a classroom during a maths exam. But even though she was extremely nervous she felt relieved that everything seemed to be working as planned. She had heard Mum and Dr D go upstairs shortly after ten as usual and after that everything had gone quiet. Only dinner had been a bit difficult.

They had all sat at the table like three strangers. Kuki had been so nervous she had hardly touched her moin-moin, which she usually loved. Dr D had tried to make some conversation but neither Kuki nor her mum had been in the mood for small talk.

'I'm so tired today,' Kuki had said after dinner. 'Can I leave the table? I'd like to go to bed early.'

Her mum had raised one eyebrow precariously high above a disbelieving eye. Kuki had bitten her lip nervously.

'Is everything really fine now at school?'

'Yes, Mum! Really! Like I already told you, I didn't even get any punishment! It was just a misunderstanding.'

'Dr D told me about the girl who has been bullying you.'

Kuki had turned to Dr D, shocked. 'I thought you didn't want us bothering Mum with all that?'

'Well, after you ran away from school and we couldn't find you I obviously had to tell your mum what I knew. I mean, we spent the evening trying to guess what might have led you to run away from school, remember?'

Kuki had nodded, feeling bad.

'I am the one disappointed here, OK?' Kuki's mum had said. 'I don't want to hear any of this talk of keeping things from Mum and not having Mum worried and all that.' She had glanced meaningfully at Dr D, who looked uncomfortable.

'I want to know everything that's happening in this house and everything going well or wrong in your life. I am not made of sugar. I want to be there for you! Give me a chance and trust me, OK?'

'OK, Mum!'

Her mum had pulled her into an embrace across the table which had been difficult with the table, the food and Mum's belly in the way.

'I'm so sorry for all the things I said that night, Mum. I didn't mean any of it.'

Kuki had held on tightly to her mum and hoped she wouldn't hurt her by what was about to happen tonight.

'I mean it, Kuki. No more secrets!'

'Only one very last secret, Mum,' she whispered now as she tiptoed to the back door, where she fumbled briefly with the key, and then slipped out quietly into the thick and heavy night. Kuki shivered as she waited in the shadows for Enilo. The estate was dark apart from two houses up the road.

Soon she saw Enilo's figure appear on the path. She waved and Kuki hurried towards her.

'The charms!' Enilo hissed, backing away. 'You were meant to wear them! You might not have time later and that would be too dangerous!'

'I know,' Kuki whispered. 'I just didn't want to wear them in the house because of the tinkling bells.'

Enilo darted down the path as soon as Kuki began to put on the bracelets and chains.

Kuki hurried after her, shining her torch this way and that to see the path but keeping her distance from Enilo, so as not to hurt her.

Now that the first and easy part was done and she had nothing else to concentrate on, she began to feel the weight of the impending task and it almost choked her. Even though she was following Enilo at a reasonable pace, Kuki felt totally out of breath. Her heart slapped against her ribcage as if it were trying to escape.

'Yes, me too,' she told her pounding heart. 'I would also love to escape if I could.'

But she knew she couldn't, and so she followed Enilo who moved swiftly and quietly like a boat on a still ocean, only her head bobbing slightly.

Much too soon, Enilo stopped and Kuki could see the metal bars of the gates.

'It is time,' Enilo said. Her voice was a broken whisper and to Kuki's shock her eyes began to glow a dim red.

Beyond the tall, foreboding gate which seemed to be warning her to turn back, the mansion loomed up against the grey night sky. Enilo slipped in through the gap and Kuki switched off her torch. She pushed it into her back pocket and gripped the metal bars. They were cold and hard as she leant her forehead against them for support. Enilo placed a finger to her lips and pointed to her wrist to remind Kuki to keep track of time. Then, like the spirit that she was, she slipped away so lightly that she seemed to float into the darkness.

Kuki's fingers immediately began to have a life of their own, trembling so hard that the gate began to vibrate. She gulped and clung more tightly to the gate to steady them. A glimpse at her watch told her it was twenty past eleven. She would give Enilo two minutes to hide upstairs. Then she would have to go in.

41

THE ATTACK

Her feet carried her like wobbly moin-moin. But even though everything inside her cried out to turn around, she plodded on, sneaking closer to the dark, grand entrance.

She could hear shrieks and a low chatter already. The Abiku were there.

Kuki swallowed and glanced up at the curved stairway. It looked like a huge, slithering snake in the darkness. Enilo would be upstairs now, waiting for her to do her part. Depending on her. While Kuki would also be depending on Enilo. Neither of them could fail!

Kuki clenched and unclenched her fists in one quick gesture and then marched forward through the house with bold, determined steps.

In the blue mosaic courtyard, the tree was a vibrating mass of leaves, branches and limbs. The spirit children were one with it. Sliding limbs and bobbing heads and trembling leaves all intertwined.

'Hey!' Kuki called with a burst of energy. 'Hey! I'm talking to you! Abiku spirits!' she called louder and was surprised at the sharpness to her voice.

The chattering in the tree stopped and there was a cold silence. A dark wind bristled through the leaves.

'Is she talking to us?' a voice in the tree whispered.

'Why can she hear us? Can she see us?'

Kuki folded her arms tightly across her chest. 'Yes, I can see and hear you! I know you have been calling Enilo away from me! I just came here to tell you that I am fighting back. I won't allow it. We are one, we are friends, and we refuse to be separated!'

After a brief moment of awkward silence there was a loud shriek.

Kuki flinched and took a careful step backwards. But then the shriek turned to laughter and the whole tree was a jumble of giggles.

'Littttle, helplesssss huuuman,' a voice said. It was slithery and smooth. So smooth that Kuki immediately felt goose pimples sprouting at the back of her neck.

'Who is Enilo, by the way?' another more childish voice asked from further behind the tree.

'Who else can it be?' another voice replied. 'Who would punish herself by giving herself a name that means "the one who went away"?'

'Ah!' many voices murmured.

'And who would be so stupid as to show herself to a human and thereby bestow upon the human the power to see and hear us? The power to see the supernatural?'

'Ah! It is our little troublemaker.'

'Silenccccce!' the slithery voice hissed and the tree hushed.

'You do not know what you say, human,' the voice continued. 'Your presence here alone shows your naivety. You think this is a game.'

'I do not think this is a game,' Kuki called, trying to make her voice sound firm, but not exactly succeeding. And then suddenly remembering why she was here, she realized she had to hurry. She had to get them angry and away from the tree as quickly as possible so Enilo would have enough time to go in, find her token shell and return before midnight. 'Mischievous, good-for-nothing spirits!' she called. 'Don't think I am afraid of you!'

Suddenly the tree lit up with red dots. It looked as if the entire tree were swarming with red fireflies.

'My name is Kokumo! And I will not die!' she cried. And as she said it she believed it with all her heart. For the first time in her life Kuki felt a strength in her that was born of her name. 'You cannot hurt me. You are nothing in the face of my name!'

The red eyes were quivering now and she could feel the anger in the air as the dark wind from the tree hit her in a heavy, cold burst.

Red dots, in pairs of two, began to drop from the tree. Kuki turned with a gasp and lunged into the house.

She stumbled through the corridor, hitting her arm painfully against the door frame. But the

Abiku were quicker and when she entered the mirrored hall she was already surrounded by a circle of red eyes, fencing her in with slow movements. Like leopards circling an antelope.

Even though she felt faint, Kuki focused and raised her arms, holding up the charms on her wrists. She shook them with all her strength and the bells rattled.

The Abiku began to crumple and writhe, holding their hands to their ears and howling.

Kuki almost covered her own ears, so awful were their shrieks. She spread her arms and swivelled around and the circle around her widened. But the moment she let her arms down they began to close in on her again. The Abiku cursed and screamed and yelled at her. She stumbled and almost fell. Kuki began to panic. Enilo couldn't come downstairs if they all remained here. And she just wanted to be back home and safe. She had to get them out to the front. But how could she get past them, break out of the circle?

She thought frantically and then, taking up her last bit of courage, she spread her arms out as wide as she could, rattling the charms wildly, and began walking towards the door that would lead her out. The horrible yelling and the wicked cursing increased, but the circle parted in front of her. The shadows fell back against the walls and she ran through the hallway and out of the door, past the dancing statues.

She ran as fast as she could, her heart thudding in rhythm with her legs. But before she could get to the gate she was surrounded again.

'Useless human! We will have our revenge on you. We will catch your Abiku. We will catch your Enilo and drag her home! She will leave you. This time for good! We will not let her return!'

Kuki tried not to look up and not to listen to their words. By now she was blinded by her tears and could hardly see a thing.

Suddenly something slammed into the back of her head. A terrible pain tore through her brain. A shower of tiny stones and gravel hit her. She yelped in pain as she slipped through the gates, sobbing breathlessly.

Kuki looked back. The gate was a mass of wriggling dark shadows and red dots.

A few more steps and she would be out of their

reach. Enilo had told her the power of the Abiku would fade the further away they were from the tree. She ran faster, heard more stones hit the ground behind her. But they didn't reach her any more. Red spots popped up in the trees above her, chasing after her, but soon faded. The wind howled with the echoes of their cries, but nothing came close to her as she ran. She was safe.

Kuki pulled out her torch from the back pocket of her jeans as she stumbled on. She had done her part. Now she could only hope that . . .

Uff . . .

Why did she suddenly feel so weak?

42

DARKNESS AND LIGHTNING

Sobbing and rustling. Darkness. Glaring light. Where was this place?

The sun shone brightly, dropping crystals of glistening rays on a colourful garden. But the garden was not filled with plants and flowers. Colourful patches of fluffy-looking crumbs criss-crossed everything. The garden was enclosed on one side by a misty blue forest and in the distance Kuki saw even more colourful plains. She shuddered. Something didn't feel right.

All of a sudden, she noticed a figure crouched between some bright bushes. Kuki squinted and held a hand to her face to shield her eyes from the brightness. It was Enilo!

Kuki tried to shout but felt weak. Why did she feel so awful?

Enilo headed through the bushes, behind a tree in bright-red bloom and disappeared out of sight. Kuki tried to follow, but her legs wouldn't do what she wanted. And why was her sight blurring?

When Kuki finally reached the tree, feeling feverish and breathless, she was stunned at the sight of the huge strange ocean in front of her. Its waves splashed in gentle swirls and the water was a creamy colour.

Tall, dark, spiky bushes framed it in groves and Enilo was nowhere to be seen. Kuki slumped down against the tree trunk. She closed her eyes and drifted back into the darkness.

Loud cries brought her back. She managed to open her eyes and through the blur she saw Enilo had emerged from the grove of spiky grass. She stood, rooted to the ground, her eyes wide with fear, as a horde of children ran towards her. When they came closer Kuki saw their faces were sharply carved into grimaces as though their wickedness was jutting out of them. The Abiku!

They looked very angry. 'We have her!' they

screamed as they ran towards Enilo, their eyes flashing.

'Run, Enilo! Run!' Kuki tried to call, but again her voice failed her.

Enilo glanced frantically at something in the palm of her hand. Kuki caught a glimpse of a small white shell. The token! She had it!

Enilo closed her palm and began to run. She was on a long winding path and Kuki could see the dark outline of another tree ahead. It looked strangely familiar with its trunk that seemed to grow out of a blue pond of mosaic. The door back to the human world! She was close, almost there!

But the children were fast. Very fast. They were closing in on her . . .

Enilo reached the tree. And in that same moment many things happened all at once.

The spirits flung themselves at Enilo, there was a thunderous cracking sound, and Kuki's view was taken away by a burst of lightning that split the tree in two.

'No!' Kuki screamed. Her eyes blurred with tears and the darkness returned.

43

WHAT IS REAL?

Kuki had switched between terrifying dreams and reality so often in the past days that when the fever finally left her, she wasn't sure what day it was or where she was. The only thing she was sure of was that something had gone terribly wrong. A strange feeling had lodged itself in her insides. She couldn't quite feel herself properly. Like when you kneel awkwardly or sit on your foot and you can't feel your foot any more. And this numbness was the entire inside of her body.

The feeling had taken a hold of her when she'd collapsed on to the floor of her room that night, not even making it back into her bed. Mum's terrified calls for Dr D the next morning had felt like a faraway sad song.

Even in the days that followed, when she grew stronger with Mum's and Dr D's teas and soups and pampering, when every sign of illness had left her, the feeling stayed. She was alive, yes, but she didn't feel right. Where was Enilo?

She had to go to the house of shells. She had to find her.

But there was no way she could go back there alone.

'Dr D, have you ever seen the abandoned old house of shells? At the end of the forest when you take the path beside our house?'

They were at the breakfast table and the air was filled with the spicy scent of fried akara, omelette and toast.

'Hmm, do you mean the old place close to the beach?'

Kuki nodded eagerly, surprised that he knew it.

'Yes, it's an abandoned estate that was in the news once. I think the family who owned it couldn't find a buyer or something. It's quite a huge stretch of land close to the beach and I think there are some ruins of an old building as well. I can't remember what the article was about but I do know there was something strange about it.'

'How come you're asking, Kuki?' her mum asked with her mouth full. 'Hmm, goodness, Dr D, this omelette is amazing, I can't get enough of it!'

'I know exactly how to make my beautiful, pregnant wife happy, don't I?'

'You sure do!'

'Ugh!' Kuki all but buried her face in her plate to avoid seeing their cheesy smiles at each other. She had balanced steaming hot, soft akaras on toast and crowned each one with a chunk of egg. Usually she loved akara for breakfast, but today she barely managed to nibble at her little pyramid.

'Someone mentioned the estate just recently,' she mumbled. 'I was just wondering, since they said it's somewhere around here.'

'Yes, I think it's somewhere down the forest path. Want to go this evening? It's time you got some fresh air anyway after being in here for almost a week. I wish I could remember what the article was about. Something weird, I remember.'

Kuki's heart flipped with excitement. This was perfect!

The house was all she could think about. Nothing made sense. If she was alive, then surely Enilo must have made it back with her token shell? But then where was she? And why did Kuki feel so strange? With Dr D and Mum she could finally go there and check. She felt hope kindle and warm her chest.

It was like she was grasping for straws but she didn't know what else to do. She had thought up hundreds of ideas, reasons why Enilo hadn't come to look for her. Had the Abiku forbidden it? Was she hurt and lying somewhere in the mansion? Did she need help?

The day couldn't go fast enough, and all afternoon she watched the clock nervously until they finally left the house.

Dr D and Mum were so wrapped up in each other and their discussions of what kind of new flooring they could put in the living room that they totally forgot about her. Dr D's idea of decorating Kuki's room had triggered all sorts of new ideas for the entire house.

Kuki didn't mind that they were absorbed in their conversation. She was much too nervous for any talking. In the forest an evening breeze caressed her newly weaved hair, but she shivered instead of feeling the cool relief after the hot day. She reached for her cornrows which she had decorated with cowrie shells. The hairstyle that Enilo loved best. The feel of the cowrie shells calmed her. *Surely everything will be fine.*

'So!' Dr D said when they came out of the forest and reached the crossroads. 'If I am not mistaken, I think we need to take this path here rather than our usual one that takes us up to the main road.'

Kuki's mum eyed the rather overgrown path and for a short moment Kuki's heart stopped at the thought of her plans scattering right here.

But then her mum shrugged and followed Dr D down the path.

Kuki stumbled along behind them with growing apprehension, and was so caught up in her thoughts that she didn't realize they had reached the house until she almost bumped into them.

'Yes, that's it,' Dr D said. 'Or at least what is left of it!'

Kuki drew a long breath as she walked past

them to peer through the gates.

What she saw was like a blow to her belly. A strangled cry came from between her clenched teeth, and she gripped the gates so hard her fingers almost caught on the rust.

The magnificent mansion, with its grand entrance, palm trees and dancing pillars, the huge door with the carved designs . . . Everything was gone!

She blinked and rubbed her eyes, but it didn't change the fact that what she was seeing was *not* what she had seen the last time and every other time she had come here. What had happened?

Instead of the majestic palm trees, decayed stumps lined the driveway that was so overgrown, there was hardly even a path through the bushes. The entire mansion was just a ruin covered with patches of moss and mushrooms. The roof had caved in and not a single pane of glass remained in any of the windows.

But the gap in the gate was still there.

She slipped through.

'Kuki, what do you think you are doing?' she heard her mum call. 'Come back here, I don't think it is safe to go in there!'

'Mum, I just want to get a little closer, I need to see something. I'll be careful,' she called, out of breath.

'OK, but D, please follow her in and make sure she doesn't do anything foolish,' she heard her mum call.

She had to see it, the tree, the spot where she had first met Enilo. Had she . . . ? She hardly dared think the words going on in her mind. Had she imagined all this?

She stood in front of the dark entrance and peered in. No, she hadn't, she couldn't have imagined it all! There were the remains of the large entrance hall and of the grand stairway. Well, without any handrails and with many steps missing, but this was the stairway she had climbed. The skeletal remains of a chandelier lay scattered in a corner of the hallway.

The smell of decay was overwhelming and she scrunched up her nose as she hurried through to the back.

'Kuki?' she heard Dr D shout. 'I don't think you should go in. We should be careful, the building might not be safe!'

But she ignored him and rushed through to the back door.

The sight was devastating. The beautiful blue-tiled mosaic was gone. A few tiny chipped tiles with faded blue patches and some shells lay scattered between dirt and leaves, and that was it. But the most shocking sight was the tree. It was split open, right down the middle. It looked like the hideous mouth of a beast, ripped open into an endless howling grimace. The branches were withered and grey and the leaves were dark, shrivelled clumps.

She felt like running up to the tree and slapping its trunk until it told her where her friend was. But she knew the tree couldn't tell her anything. It was dead.

The bushes had grown in so close to the tree, as if they had tried to overgrow it and cover up any last proof that the Abiku had ever existed. And that was when Kuki realized: they were all truly gone. Every single one of those wicked Abiku. And they could never hurt anyone again. Enilo had succeeded. She had closed the door for ever.

Kuki let out a choked gasp.

'You did it, Enilo,' she whispered. 'But what happened? Why am I still alive but you are not here?'

She looked around and it was as if the ruins were trying to give her the answers. The house was gone, the tree was gone. Enilo was gone.

Kuki's lips quivered and she closed her eyes. She didn't want to see the answers. She leant forward to rest her trembling hands on her knees.

Dr D came out behind her and placed a hand on her shoulder. 'Everything OK? You seem very taken by this place.'

She nodded faintly and stood up.

'It has a haunted feel about it, don't you think?' he said. 'Come to think of it, I think that was what I read in the article. Something about rumours that the place was haunted by Abiku . . .' His voice trailed away and Kuki felt him turn to gaze intently at her.

'Is that why you wanted to come here?' He looked worried.

'The Abiku don't matter now,' she said. 'They are gone and can't hurt anyone any more.' She ignored the sharp pain that came along with this realization. She'd lost Enilo.

Dr D looked at her strangely. 'What do you mean?'

She ignored his question and instead asked: 'This world, the things we see . . . do you some-times feel that they are not real?'

He didn't reply immediately. 'I think life is a journey of discovery. Of making sense of many things we don't understand. I don't think we need to understand everything, Kuki.'

'But I want to,' she cried angrily, tears seeping out of her eyes. 'I want to understand everything! Why does nothing ever make sense?'

44

AN UNEXPECTED GUEST

'Kuki, there's a girl at the door!' Her mum stuck her head through the door of her bedroom, where Kuki lay reading listlessly.

She looked up, not sure she'd understood well.

'You have a visitor!' Her mum was beaming.

Kuki grew rigid. Then her heart began to beat in excitement. Could it be Enilo?

She jumped out of bed and charged across the room, squeezing past her mum.

'Careful now, slowly, hon. You were ill for almost a week, you shouldn't be too—'

But Kuki was already at the end of the corridor and running into the living room. She wasn't listening.

At the door she stopped abruptly, blinking her

eyes in irritation.

Moji was standing at the door.

Kuki stared in confusion.

Moji stared back, her arms folded across her chest.

Kuki frowned. She would have expected to see anyone really, but definitely not Moji. She was deeply disappointed. And she didn't feel like talking to anyone. She just wanted Enilo back!

'Hi,' she said stiffly.

'I have your homework,' Moji said. 'The teachers asked who lives near your place and everyone pointed at me.' She handed her a bunch of papers.

'Oh! Thank you.'

'I . . . heard you were ill.'

Kuki nodded.

'Are you OK now?'

'Yes, thanks.'

There was an awkward silence.

Kuki fidgeted with the papers, wondering what Moji wanted. She was obviously not ready to leave yet. Kuki felt nervous as she watched her from the corner of her eye. Moji was staring at the ground and pushing her foot around as if she was drawing imaginary circles.

'Nobody in school talks to me any more,' Moji said.

'I'm sorry about that.'

Moji glanced up sharply. 'Really?'

'Yes, I didn't mean for things to come to this.'

'It's your fault though!' Moji hissed suddenly.

'No, it's not, and you know it.' Kuki was surprised at the firmness in her voice. She wasn't afraid. The past few days and weeks had moulded a different person out of her. She'd faced evil spirits. Moji was nothing.

'You could at least try to be nice to me, now that everyone is mean. You owe me!'

'If you shout at me and try to boss me around, I will definitely not be nice to you. I do not owe you anything. And I won't let you bully me around any more.' Now it was Kuki who crossed her arms.

Moji stared at her angrily. Then her eyes suddenly drooped and the anger was gone. She looked sad now. And lonely. Kuki felt sorry. If there was a list of people who knew what feeling lonely and not having friends meant then she was definitely on that list!

'I . . .' Kuki cleared her throat. 'I want you to know that I think you have good sides as well. I know that didn't really come across in the biography, but that was obviously because I was angry and hurt. You really weren't nice to me. Or to most kids in class!'

Moji looked dejected again. She shuffled her feet uneasily. She was wearing her usual sandals and her feet were big and awkward in them. Then her face brightened hopefully. 'In the biography, you said I could have much better grades if I wanted to. Do you really think so?'

'Of course! You can be clever when you want to be,' Kuki said.

'No one has ever thought I am clever. Not even my parents.'

'Well, you were smart enough to get the whole class doing what you wanted! Not everybody can do that, you know,' Kuki said. 'The problem is you use your good sides for the wrong things, like making someone else do your homework.' She raised an eyebrow meaningfully.

'We could learn together!'

'What?' Kuki asked.

'Since we live on the same street, we could learn together or do homework together.'

'Ehm . . .' Kuki stammered, not feeling too sure about the idea.

'Please, Kuki, I need to improve my grades. I really can't repeat another class.'

Kuki still didn't reply.

'I promise I'll be nice. You're so smart with school stuff, Kuki, please will you help me?' Moji stared at her hands. 'I'm sorry, Kuki. I know I was really mean to you.'

Kuki drew a long breath. The biography had not been very nice either and even though she hadn't planned for it to be read to the entire class, she felt responsible for the catastrophe that had followed.

'OK,' she said.

45

STAY WITH ME

Kuki walked down the school steps after closing bell and it was the strangest of things that she wasn't walking alone. Faith was walking beside her, chattering something about Sahid.

'I'm telling you, he has a crush on you, Kuki!'

Kuki laughed it off, feeling embarrassed. She still had to get used to the new way everyone in class saw her. Like she was some kind of hero. She wasn't really sure she liked all the attention, but she definitely enjoyed being a part of everything now and not being the class outcast. Moji was already waiting impatiently for them at the gate. A different Moji, who had begun to laugh and smile more often instead of sneering. It was as if the weight of all the lying and pretending had eased and made her a happier person. She only bossed others around once in a while through habit, but when she did everyone just ignored her.

The strange numbness inside Kuki had not entirely gone. She thought of Enilo every single day and missed her terribly, but slowly the numbness had begun to feel a tiny bit less intense, less hurtful.

'So should we go to your place or my place today?' Moji asked Kuki.

'Oh, please, let's go to yours again, Moji,' Faith said. 'I want to play with your fluffy cat.' Moji's eyes lit up and she nodded. 'If that's OK for Kuki?'

But Kuki didn't reply. She was running towards Dr D, whom she'd spotted standing outside the gate. Her heart raced as a wave of confusion and fear took over. But then she saw his wide grin.

'You have a baby brother!' he called. Without even thinking, Kuki jumped into his arms with an excited squeal.

The smell of hospital air was sharp, clean and pungent. Kuki sped up the steps behind Dr D, two at a time. Her heart thumped with an irregular talking-drum kind of beat. As if her heart were drumming a message to her.

'I know,' she whispered to it as she pushed through the door that Dr D held open.

Her mum was in the first bed and she was holding a tiny bundle to her chest and beaming.

'Your big sister is here,' she said to the bundle when she saw Kuki.

Kuki hurriedly washed her hands in the basin near the door like Dr D had done.

'Mum!' was all she could say in a whisper when she saw him. He was beautiful. With shiny black hair and large eyes that were half closed. He made tiny noises and waved his cute arms around as if he were doing gymnastics.

'Do you want to hold him?' Mum asked.

Kuki nodded and sat down on the chair beside the bed. Her mum placed the tiny bundle in her arms. The soft blue blanket slipped off his legs and exposed the tiniest, cutest feet she had ever seen.

'Oh, Mum, he is so precious,' she said, covering him up again. But she stopped abruptly when she saw a small birthmark close to his ankle. It was light in colour, lighter than the rest of his brown skin. And it had a strange shape. Kuki's heart seemed to stop beating altogether as she stared at it in recognition.

'Looks like a seashell, don't you think?' her mum said with a smile.

Kuki nodded, her eyes brimming over with tears. It *was* a seashell!

Enilo!

She had made it back! She had come back with her little brother. And she had brought back her lucky shell with her.

Kuki gasped at the realization and hugged the little bundle closer.

She hadn't entirely lost her dearest friend. Enilo was free! And she had become what she had always wanted to be. A good spirit. She was a beautiful pearl tucked safely in an oyster's shell. At last she had found a home.

'Where is my nephew?' a familiar voice called much too loudly. The other women in the two other beds looked up as Aunty breezed in, her bright jewellery glittering on her neck and wrists.

'What a wonderful day, congratulations to my brother and thank you for making me a proud aunty of a niece and now a nephew!' Aunty cried, her eyes beaming and full of tears.

Kuki watched her hug Dr D and then go on to hug her mum. She was glad to see there were no hard feelings. Now that her little brother was born and obviously healthy and well, Kuki hoped Aunty would stop all the talk about the Abiku. And now that the door to their world was gone, maybe soon people would notice that the Abiku were truly gone. No one would ever suffer again and the story of the Abiku would soon really be just an old myth.

'What is his name?' Aunty asked, gently placing a hand on Kuki's shoulder and peering over.

'Rotimi!' Kuki said proudly, repeating the name Dr D had told her in the car on the way to the hospital.

'Oh, what a beautiful and perfect name,' Aunty cried and clapped her hands in glee. 'You know what it means, Kokumo?'

Kuki nodded.

'It means "stay with me"!'

She smiled at her brother and felt a deep calm.

Yes, the name was perfect, she thought as she traced the outline of his beautiful birthmark. Rotimi had definitely come to stay.

AUTHOR'S NOTE

Folk tales and myths have always fascinated me. In Nigeria we have myriads of intriguing tales of haunted trees and spirits, cursed families, magical realms, deities and wise tortoises, which I loved as a child but unfortunately hardly found in books. But luckily, in the late 80s/90s we had a wonderful show on Nigerian TV for kids called *Tales by Moonlight*, which featured traditional folklore told in the storytelling style of the olden days. And of course, every child had an aunt or their parents, a neighbour or a wise grandmother who told them a tale or two. Tales which have been told for generations on moonlit nights, some cited in verse or accompanied by songs in call and response custom. Many of them told with a clear warning that they are true.

The tale of the Abiku is one of the most persistent. The spirit child that plagues cursed families by being born again and again into the same family. The Abiku deliberately dies at a young age, usually before puberty, causing a lot of sorrow, only to be reborn again to continue the cycle. The

Abiku exist across different Nigerian cultures, sometimes bearing other names like Ogbanje, but whatever the name or the nuances of their story, the common tie is the mischievous nature of these spirit children and the havoc they cause.

Modern theories suggest that the concept of the Abiku is a mythological explanation for certain hereditary diseases like sickle cell anaemia, which led to multiple deaths of children within the same family.

However, modern studies have not managed to wipe out the fascination with the concept and the belief in the Abiku. The story of the spirit child lives on, still often told with a warning that it is true. That the Abiku exist.

I have always longed to see our Nigerian myths and folk tales transported into books for children. We have our own wonderfully magical stories to tell. We should ask the older generations for more of them and write them down quickly before they are forgotten.

ACKNOWLEDGEMENTS

Heartfelt thanks to my family. My mum, to whom I owe my love for books and who does night shifts if necessary to read my drafts. My dad, for his unwavering faith in us.

My wonderful, flag-waving husband, who has managed to tell more people about my book than I could have thought possible, and my three daughters, my gems and biggest cheerleaders. Thank you for making me feel so special and for being patient and forgiving when I have my busy writing phases. The thing is, I'm the one who is so proud to have you in my life!

My lovely Sisterly, Elele, who listened to all my thoughts, questions and worries at the beginning of the book and helped me sort them out. My two awesome brothers Odia and Osebo who are always there for me, in all my wild endeavours.

And thank you to my dear brother-in-law Dayo, my Yoruba expert, always ready to throw over a translation or explanation.

A huge thank you to Rachel Leyshon, my brilliant editor, for immediately loving the story idea and encouraging me to write the book. For her thought-provoking questions, spot-on ideas and her infectious excitement about shells.

A loud, enthusiastic shout to Jazz Bartlett Love for always making me and my books shine out there.

Thank you, Elinor Bagenal, for listening to my heart's desire and ensuring my books found their way to Nigeria. To Rachel Hickman for all the absolutely fantastic cover details and to Barry Cunningham for his thoughtful and wise feedback.

To all the other lovely people at Chicken House: Olivia Jeggo, Laura Myers, Esther Waller, Sarah Wallis-Newman and Kesia Lupo, and to Sue Cook. Thank you all for helping to make this book come true.

A special thank you to Adamma Okonkwo for her awesome and accurate sensitivity check and for the touching feedback.

You did it again, lovely Helen Crawford-White! You made me another beautiful cover that says it all. Thank you.

A huge thank you to my agent Clare Wallace

for championing me and making me feel heard all the way from Germany to the UK, and that, in a pandemic.

Thank you Othuke Ominiabohs at Masobe Books – for bringing my stories home, and with so much love and enthusiasm. This means a lot to me.

To Mr Akinte and Mrs Agbi in the book, who represent two teachers who inspired me with their enthusiasm and love for their work.

To all my new author and book friends, especially to Richard Pickard and to Alexandra Page. For sharing their authorly thoughts, advice and excitements with me.

Thank you to all the book-loving people out there. Kids and adults, teachers, bloggers and booksellers. For all the love and support, which has been overwhelming.

I truly believe that books can change lives, especially for children. As an author, being told that my book has in some way, no matter how small, touched someone, changes my life every time, making me want to be an author all over again.

Thank you!

Lines from 'Abiku' by Wole Soyinka, copyright © Wole Soyinka 1967, from *Idanre and Other Poems* (Methuen, 1967), are used by permission of the author through the Melanie Jackson Agency, LLC.

ALSO BY EFUA TRAORÉ

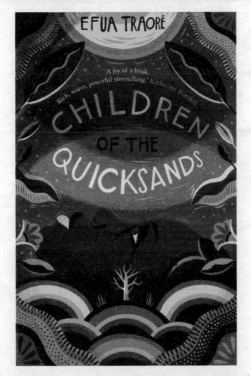

CHILDREN OF THE QUICKSANDS

Simi is sent to stay with her long-lost grandmother in a remote Nigerian village. There's no TV, internet or phone. Not a single human sound can be heard at night, just the noise of birds and animals in the dark forest.

Her grandmother makes herbal medicines for the villagers, but she won't talk to Simi about their family's past. Something bad must have happened, but what? To find out, Simi goes exploring.

Caught in the sinking red quicksand of a forbidden lake, her extraordinary journey begins . . .

'A joy of a book. Rich, warm, powerful storytelling.'
KATHERINE RUNDELL

Paperback, ISBN 978-1-913322-36-6, £7.99 • ebook, ISBN 978-1-913696-05-4, £7.99